DEATH BECOMES YOU

DEANNA LYNN SLETTEN

Death Becomes You
A Rachel Emery Novel
Book Two

Copyright 2021 © Deanna Lynn Sletten

This is a work of fiction. Names, characters, places, and incidents are either the product of the author's imagination or are used fictitiously, and any resemblance to any actual persons, living or dead, events, or locales is entirely coincidental.

ISBN 13: 978-1-941212-62-2

Cover Designer: Deborah Bradseth of Tugboat Design

DEATH
BECOMES
YOU

CHAPTER ONE

Rachel Emery sat at her desk, working on a romance novel cover for one of her authors. It had been a beautiful November day in Tallahassee, and peaceful, which was fine with Rachel. After the hectic time she'd had in California in September proving she was still alive, she looked forward to the quiet. Rachel was finishing up work for the week and planned on visiting her Aunt Julie the next day for lunch. After that, she was meeting her daughter, Jules, for dinner and a movie. She looked forward to a normal day with her family.

Her phone buzzed, pulling Rachel out of her thoughts. She glanced at it and smiled. It was Ariel Weathers, one of her clients. Rachel generally didn't give out her number to clients because she preferred to correspond by text or email. But Arial, a romance novelist she'd been working with for over four years, was different. Rachel enjoyed talking with her. She was witty and knowledgeable, and she always trusted Rachel to create the perfect designs for her.

"Hi, Ariel. How are you?" Rachel said.

"Oh, Rachel. I'm so sorry to bother you. But I had to call. I desperately need your help." Ariel sounded anxious.

Rachel was surprised. Ariel wrote drama, but she didn't play at it. So, if she was upset, there had to be a good reason. "What's wrong?"

"I thought you could help me. I mean, after what happened to you and how you solved the mystery of your supposed death, well, I thought you could do the same for me. I really don't know who else to turn to." Ariel's words were rushed as if she were nervous.

"Well, I'm not a professional investigator," Rachel said. "But I can try to help."

"My ex-husband, who died in a boating accident almost a year ago, is stalking me. I think he wants to kill me. I'm scared out of my mind. Will you help?"

Rachel pulled the phone away from her ear and stared at it, stunned. Would she help? She knew she should say no, but now, she was intrigued.

* * *

"Her dead ex-husband is stalking her?" Jules stared wide-eyed at her mother. Her expression almost made Rachel laugh. Her nineteen-year-old daughter was usually so calm and unflappable, but the crazy story Rachel had dropped on her was pretty shocking.

"That's what Ariel said," Rachel told Jules as she took a bite of her grilled chicken. It was Saturday evening, and they'd met for dinner and planned to go to a movie afterward. "Her ex-husband, Randall, died over eight months ago when his yacht blew up in the Gulf. Now, she keeps seeing him. She's afraid he faked his death and is now after her to get the life insurance money."

Jules pushed back her long, auburn hair and took a bite of her burger. "That sounds like something crazy from a thriller movie. How could he fake his death? Didn't they need to prove he was dead before they paid her the insurance money?"

Rachel shrugged. They were sitting outside on the restaurant's patio, and a gust of wind came up suddenly. She slipped her dark hair back behind her ears, out of her face. Since returning from California, Rachel had let her hair grow longer, and it was now almost as long as her daughter's. But the two women couldn't have looked more different from each other. Rachel's five-foot, seven-inch height was no match to Jules's tall, slender frame. Jules was wearing skinny jeans and heels that made her legs look endless. Rachel was no slouch, but next to her daughter, she felt short.

"I don't know all the details. I told Ariel I'd visit her tomorrow at her house, and we could talk more about it," Rachel said. "She was nervous about discussing it over the phone."

"You'll have to let me know what she says," Jules said. She cocked her brow at her mother. "She's not a kook, is she?"

Rachel laughed. "I never thought she was before. We'll see after tomorrow."

As they ate, they talked about Jules' college classes and her friend, Amber, who roomed with her at the nice off-campus apartment they shared. Then Jules asked about her mother's visit with Julie earlier in the day.

Rachel sighed. "Your Aunt Julie isn't doing very well. Her memory is getting worse. She didn't recognize me until I was almost ready to leave after lunch. Shirley, her caretaker at the memory unit, said her memory has been in and out. Julie doesn't even remember Shirley sometimes."

"That's so sad," Jules said. "I should go and see her again

soon. It's hard when she doesn't know who you are, though."

"It is. I had hoped Julie's new medication would help her, but it doesn't seem to be working. I was so hoping I could tell her I know the truth now—about her being my biological mother. I think if she were thinking clearly, she'd be relieved I finally know. But in her state of mind, it would only upset her."

Rachel had unraveled the family secret when she'd returned to her hometown of Casita, California in September to prove she was alive. Everyone had thought she was the girl in the grave from thirty-five years earlier when the truth was her aunt and uncle had taken her away all those years ago. After solving the mystery, Rachel had learned that her Aunt Julie and Uncle Gordon were her actual parents, which was why they'd taken her. Now, with her Uncle Gordon deceased and her Aunt Julie suffering from Alzheimer's, Rachel couldn't let her know that she'd learned the truth.

"I'm sorry, Mom," Jules said sympathetically. "But at least you know the truth."

Rachel agreed. She was no longer in the dark about her family's history.

They left soon afterward and went to see a romantic comedy. It was fun relaxing with her daughter and forgetting about everything. Two hours later, Rachel said goodbye to Jules and headed back to her home a half-hour away.

As she crawled into bed, Rachel's phone buzzed. She glanced at it and smiled. Avery Turley, the man she'd met in California in September who'd helped her solve the mystery of the murdered girl, had texted her. They'd become very close during the investigation but unfortunately hadn't been able to find a weekend when they both could get away and see each other. He was an FBI agent at a bureau in Maryland, and his job kept him busy around the clock.

"Hope you had a fun time with Jules at the movies. Hopefully, we can grab a movie together sometime soon," Avery texted.

"I hope so too," Rachel texted back. *"I'll call you tomorrow night and let you know what's new. Something interesting has happened."*

"Hopefully, nothing dangerous," Avery texted.

She laughed. After nearly being shot and having her head smashed in with a rock in September, meeting with Ariel was not even close to dangerous.

"No. Not dangerous."

"Goodnight."

Rachel texted goodnight, too, and set her phone down. She missed Avery. He was the first man she'd become involved with since her husband, Carter, had died four years earlier. She really hoped to see Avery soon.

"But first, I have to find out about the dead ex-husband stalking Ariel," she said to herself.

* * *

Sunday morning, Rachel drove her Honda CRV in the rain the two hours it took to reach Ariel's Panama City home. Luckily, the downpour had cleared by the time she drove into the elegant neighborhood and pulled into Ariel's driveway.

Rachel glanced around the quiet street. Ariel's home had an island look to it with a long, covered porch and two large willow trees shading the front lawn. Each yard was separated by tall brick walls and had carefully manicured green lawns. It was a beautiful, suburban neighborhood, and Rachel couldn't imagine anyone feeling unsafe here.

Grabbing her purse, Rachel walked up to the front door where she noticed a security camera hidden under the eaves. It was warm out, but they weren't far from the Gulf of Mexico, and she felt its cooling breeze. She'd worn jeans and a light cotton shirt with flat sandals and hoped she hadn't under-dressed now that she'd seen how nice Ariel's house was. Before Rachel even touched the doorbell, Ariel threw the door open.

"Oh, Rachel! I'm so glad you're here. Come in," Ariel exclaimed, clearly thrilled to see her.

The two women embraced, and then Rachel followed her into the large, spacious living room. The home had tall, beamed ceilings with tropical fans up high and beautiful hard-wood flooring all around. The kitchen and dining room were open to the living room, and across the way, out the large patio windows, Rachel saw a sparkling built-in pool and hot tub surrounded by a flowering garden.

"Your house is gorgeous!" Rachel said, glancing around. The kitchen had white cabinets with black granite countertops. Off the dining room was another space through French doors that looked like an office.

"Oh, thank you, dear," Ariel said, leading her to the kitchen counter and offering her a seat. "We've lived here for ten years and just love it." She worried her lip with her teeth. "Well, I live here alone now, but Randall and I bought this right after we were married. It's only a short drive to the marina where he kept his yacht."

Rachel nodded, not sure how to respond. She didn't know whether or not they'd had an amicable divorce. Assuming Ariel thought he was out to kill her, it couldn't have been too friendly.

"Can I offer you a drink? Soda? Iced tea? I just made a fresh pitcher of sweet tea."

"That sounds wonderful," Rachel said. She watched as Ariel dropped ice into tall crystal glasses and then poured the tea from a slender pitcher. Everything in the kitchen was just as beautiful and pristine as the rest of the house—just as Ariel was. Ariel was nearly a decade younger than Rachel at age thirty-four and was the same height. She was a natural blonde with a head of thick hair cut into a swingy bob, and her skin was nearly translucent. Her ice-blue eyes shone bright, and she was as slender as a fashion model. Ariel moved like a lithe dancer and dressed artfully—the only word Rachel could think of to describe Ariel's style. While she wore skinny jeans, a flowery blouse, and tall espadrilles, it was the carefully applied makeup and many rings, bracelets, and necklaces she wore that gave Rachel the artsy impression.

Ariel's many bracelets jangled now as she set the sweet tea in front of Rachel on the counter. "Let's sit in the living room. It's more comfortable," Ariel said, and Rachel followed her there with her drink in hand.

Once seated on the flowery cushions of the heavy wooden furniture, Rachel asked, "Why don't we start at the beginning? Why do you think your ex-husband faked his death?"

A long sigh escaped Ariel's pouty red lips. She reached for one of her necklaces and toyed with the golden sun charm. "About two years ago, my book sales began to soar, which I thought was wonderful after only five years of self-publishing. Suddenly, we had more money than we'd ever dreamed possible, and for some unknown reason, that bothered Randall. He'd always thought of my writing as a fun hobby—never as a way to actually earn a livable income. He was an investment broker and had always earned a good income. I think my having money scared him a little."

Rachel frowned. "Why? Was he jealous?"

"Oh, no. I don't think so. More like he felt less like a man if he didn't earn all the money in the relationship." Ariel sighed dramatically. "I don't understand it. It was soon after that he began going to bars and having affairs with younger women, and I was just beside myself. It made no sense to me. We'd been so happy together, and he just snapped one day and changed completely."

"That's awful," Rachel said, reaching out and placing a comforting hand on Ariel's arm. "I'm so sorry. Is that what led to the divorce?"

Ariel nodded, her topaz earrings bobbing with her head. "I had worked too hard to give up my writing career just to save his male ego. And I could never live with a man who cheated. So, I kicked him out, changed the locks, and put up a camera system around the house. He was furious but finally accepted that we were through."

"Relationships are difficult," Rachel said sympathetically. "I'm sorry it came to that. How did he behave after the divorce? Was he angry or vengeful?"

Ariel took a sip of her drink and then placed it carefully on the glass-topped coffee table. "He tried to get back together, then gave up. Randall moved onto his yacht, and from what I heard from other friends, began throwing parties and hanging out at the bar at the marina with a different girl each night." Ariel's eyes filled with tears. "It hurt. I loved him so much. We married when we both were twenty-four and were so in love. We did everything together—Caribbean vacations, boating for weeks at a time—everything. It never made sense why he suddenly changed."

Rachel picked up a box of tissues from the end table and

set them next to Ariel, who dabbed at her eyes, careful not to smudge her mascara.

"Randall was such a handsome man. I can't blame women for flocking to him," Ariel said. "And he's smart—really smart. He always bragged he was smarter than me, and that never bothered me because I believed it was true. But as my career escalated and I was managing advertising and marketing, I think he saw that I was no dummy, and that bothered him. I guess he just wanted a woman who hung on his every word as if it were gospel."

Rachel had known men like that through the years. Ones that based their masculinity on being more intelligent than their wives. She had been thankful her husband had been proud of the work she did. Carter had been a good man and father. Even after four years, she still missed him.

"But then he died in the boating accident," Rachel said to urge Ariel forward. "How did that happen?"

She shook her head. "No one knows why his boat blew up. It could have been a defect in the engine, or it could have been a gas leak. After digging into his work life, one investigator even thought a client who'd lost money on investments may have rigged the boat to catch fire. Can you believe that? It's like something from a cheesy novel."

"But they proved he actually died in the explosion?" Rachel asked.

"Yes, they did. I had some of his personal effects that they were able to get a DNA match from. There wasn't much of him to find." Tears filled her eyes again. "It was so gruesome. But they did identify him." Ariel began wringing her hands. "That's what makes this all so insane. How could he be dead but still be showing up, stalking me? I see him everywhere!"

"Where have you seen Randall?" Rachel asked calmly, trying to soothe Ariel's strained nerves.

Ariel glanced nervously out the patio windows, then leaned in closer toward Rachel. "Everywhere," she whispered. "In the grocery store. At the beach. Last night, I saw him in the back-yard, standing by the pool. He was just staring at me through the window." She shivered. "I feel like I'm losing my mind."

Rachel felt a chill run up her spine just thinking about what Ariel had thought she'd seen. It had to be unnerving to see her dead ex-husband, even if it might be her imagination. "What do you think he wants?" she asked Ariel.

Ariel stared at her and frowned. "Don't you understand? He's come back for the money. He wants the two-million dollars and will do anything in his power to get it."

CHAPTER TWO

Rachel stared at Ariel, speechless. Two-million dollars? That was a large sum of money. "Where did the money come from?" Rachel asked.

"Randall's life insurance policy," Ariel said matter-of-factly. Her fearfulness from just moments before had vanished. "While we were married, we each had a large insurance policy in case one of us died. Randall wanted to make sure I was taken care of if something happened to him and vice-versa. After we divorced, we kept paying for the policies. I collected the money two months ago after the police determined Randall had died on the boat. I also got a big check from the insurance for the boat."

Rachel pondered that a moment. Two-million dollars. It was enough to make anyone want to come back from the dead. "Have you been contacted by anyone about giving up the money?"

Ariel looked at her blankly. "No. You mean like someone blackmailing me?"

Rachel nodded. "You know for certain your ex-husband is dead, so maybe someone else is impersonating him to try to get the money from you."

Ariel's eyes lit up, and she grabbed Rachel's hands. "So, you do believe that I'm seeing my dead ex-husband? Thank goodness. My sister keeps telling me I'm imagining it, and I've been so scared to tell anyone else."

Rachel gave her a small smile. "Of course, I believe you're seeing someone. But it may not be him. I noticed you have a security camera in front. Have you caught the person on any of your cameras?"

Ariel's head bobbed up and down. "I have. Come, I'll show you." She stood and lead Rachel through the French doors to her office and headed for the computer. "It's clearer on my computer screen than on my phone," Ariel explained. Sitting at the heavy wooden desk, she began typing on her laptop.

Rachel glanced around the room as she waited for Ariel to bring up the footage. It was a lovely office with glass shelving and wooden cabinets. Ariel's books were lined up on a shelf, showing off her many covers—covers Rachel had created. She moved closer to the cabinet and saw a row of photos. There were many of Ariel with a tall, handsome man with sandy blond hair and piercing blue eyes. His deep tan showed he spent a lot of time on his boat. As Rachel moved from photo to photo, she saw another of two women who looked incredibly alike, except one had blond hair and one had red. She realized it was Ariel and her sister.

"Are you and your sister twins?" Rachel asked. Except for the red hair, green eyes, and freckles, the other girl looked exactly like Ariel.

"Yes, we're identical twins," Ariel said offhandedly. "We're exactly alike except for our hair and eyes and the fact that Alivia doesn't protect her pale skin from the sun. Freckles are a red head's enemy." Ariel rolled her eyes. "Alivia lives in my guest house in the back yard and works as my assistant."

Rachel studied the photo. "I didn't know identical twins could have different hair and eye colors."

Ariel glanced up. "Yeah. It's rare, but it happens. Something to do with gene mutation. Here, I have the video ready."

Rachel placed the photo back on the cabinet and walked around behind Ariel. The video began playing, and Rachel saw Ariel's ex-husband, plain as day, standing beside the pool in the moonlight. The video was so clear, there was no mistaking who it was.

"Well, what do you think?" Ariel asked, looking up at Rachel expectantly.

"You're right. The man looks exactly like your ex-husband. It's incredible," Rachel said.

"See. I'm not crazy. I'm seeing him. And he's stalking me. What can I do?" Ariel asked, looking anxious.

Rachel walked slowly around the desk again and stared at the photos of Ariel and her ex-husband. There was no doubt he was the man in the video. She turned back to Ariel. "You should take a copy of that video to the police. If Randall isn't dead, they should know, especially if he means to harm you."

Ariel drooped like a wilted flower. "I can't go to the police," she said pitifully.

Rachel frowned. "Why not?"

She raised her blue eyes to Rachel. "Because if the police learn that my ex-husband is alive—and that he may have faked his death—they'll implicate me in the scheme. I'm the one who profited from his death. There's no way they'd believe I wasn't in on it."

Rachel moved closer to the desk. "Were you in on it?" She hated asking the question, but she needed to know the truth.

Ariel jolted and sat up straight. "No! I could never have done such a thing. Please, believe me, Rachel. I honestly believed Randall died on that boat. They matched his DNA. How could he possibly still be alive?"

Rachel nodded. "I do believe you. But I had to ask." She moved a chair from the corner up to the front of the desk and sat. "What do you want me to do?"

Ariel looked relieved that Rachel believed her. "Would you look into the case and see if you can find any evidence that Randall faked his death? Discreetly, of course. Maybe study the newspaper and police reports. Maybe you'll catch something I've missed. Anything you can learn might be helpful. If I can prove Randall faked his death without my knowledge, then I can go to the police."

Rachel sat there a moment, thinking about what Ariel was asking her to do. The last time she started digging into a case, she turned a town and her life upside-down. She didn't need a dead guy stalking her, either. "I suppose I could do a little investigating, but I can't promise I'll find anything," she told Ariel.

Ariel's face brightened. "I have some of the newspaper clippings in a file here." She bent over to dig in her desk drawer.

As Ariel searched, Rachel glanced at the paperwork on her desk. There were notes for the novel she was working on in a pile by her computer. Next to it was a contract from a real estate company in the Bahamas, with a photo of a beautiful beach house. Was Ariel buying a house in the Bahamas?

"Here's the file of clippings," Ariel said, setting it in front of Rachel. "And here's a card from the officer in charge of investigating Randall's death. He was a nice man. Maybe he could get you copies of the police reports."

"Okay. I'll look through these and let you know what I come up with. Is there anything else I should know?" Rachel asked.

Ariel's brows furrowed as she thought. "You might want to check out the marina where Randall docked his boat. He'd been living on it since we'd broken up. Maybe someone down there might know something too. It's called Shady Cove Marina. There's a nice restaurant and bar there that Randall used to frequent. I'll write down the address." She picked up a Post-it note and scribbled an address, then handed it to Rachel. "And there's one more thing," Ariel said, reaching into the desk's middle drawer. She pulled out a slip of paper and handed it to Rachel. "I don't expect you to do this for free. I know you're busy. So, I'd like to pay you up-front."

Rachel looked down at the check. It was made out to her for two thousand dollars. "I can't take your money," Rachel protested.

"Please. Take it," Ariel pleaded. "I'm taking you away from your work to investigate. You deserve every cent."

"But what if I don't learn anything new?" Rachel asked.

"Then it was worth the money to know I didn't miss anything." Ariel smiled. "I so appreciate your help. Please, take the payment."

Rachel felt awkward taking the money from Ariel, but she nodded and slipped it into the folder of newspaper clippings. "Thank you. I'll see what I can find out."

Ariel came around the desk and hugged her. "You're doing me a great favor. Thank you!"

Rachel glanced down at the photo of the beach house again. Her curiosity was getting the better of her. "Beautiful beach house," she said. "Are you going on a vacation?"

Ariel glanced at the photo. "Oh, that," she said, suddenly taken off guard. She sighed dreamily. "Randall and I used to go to the Caribbean all the time on his boat, and we loved it so much, we'd planned on buying a vacation home there. But then we separated, and that was that. I decided to move ahead and buy a house on my own. I'll always think of him whenever I go there." Her eyes had a faraway look in them.

"That's nice," Rachel said. She didn't begrudge her friend for buying such a beautiful house, but she knew now where part of the life insurance money was going.

"Well, I should head home," Rachel said. "It's a long drive back to my house."

"Thank you so much for coming. Maybe you could plan to stay a few days at a nice hotel on the beach so you can investigate. I'd be happy to pay your expenses," Ariel said.

"That's a good idea. I may take you up on it," Rachel said. She turned to walk back into the living room and practically bumped into the spitting image of Ariel.

"Oh, my goodness," Rachel said, placing a hand over her heart. "I didn't hear you come in."

"That's my sister for you," Ariel said, rolling her eyes. "She floats around here. Rachel, this is Alivia. Alivia, this is Rachel."

Alivia smiled at Rachel and offered her hand. "Sorry I scared you."

Rachel shook Alivia's hand as she gazed into her deep green eyes. Her hair was dark red and cut in the same bob as Ariel's, and she had a spray of freckles across her nose and cheeks. "It's nice to meet you, Alivia."

"It's nice to meet you too," Alivia said. She looked past Rachel to her sister. "I just came in to see if you have anything for me to do today."

Ariel waved her hand dismissively through the air. "Not right now. Let me say goodbye to Rachel, and then I'll find something for you to do."

Alivia shrugged and drifted off toward the kitchen.

"Relatives," Ariel said under her breath as she walked Rachel to the door. "I promised my mother I'd take care of my sister, but sometimes it's so annoying."

"Well, it's nice that you help her out," Rachel said, trying to stay neutral.

The two women hugged goodbye, and Rachel promised to stay in touch before heading to her car. After Ariel closed the door, Rachel turned and looked up at the camera under the eaves. She wondered what else the cameras had caught and if Ariel would let her look through the videos.

Clutching the file folder to her chest, Rachel walked to her car.

* * *

That evening, Rachel called Avery to tell him about her new case.

"Are you trying to put me out of business?" he teased. "If you solve all the murders, what's left for the FBI?"

Rachel laughed. She loved her easy relationship with Avery.

"I think your job is safe," she told him. "And I wouldn't do this except Ariel is a friend, and she was so upset. But I guess if your dead ex-husband is stalking you, you would be scared."

"So, you think that was actually him on the backyard camera?" Avery asked.

"If it wasn't, then it was his twin. The video was crystal clear."

"Would you like me to do some digging into his background?

Maybe there was a reason for him to fake his death other than for the money," Avery said.

"What kind of reason?" she asked, intrigued.

"He had a boat with access to the Gulf of Mexico and the Caribbean. He may have gotten mixed up in the drug trade or worse yet, human trafficking."

"Wow. Your mind goes directly to the worst-case scenario, doesn't it? I wouldn't have thought of those things."

Avery laughed. "Sorry. It's the job. You almost always think the worse."

"If you have time to check on him, I'd appreciate it," Rachel said seriously. "But don't if you're already too busy at work."

"Yeah, right. I was gone for so long from the main office that they're making up for my absence by giving me all the paperwork. All I've been doing for weeks is helping other investigators track down leads for their investigations. Boring!"

This made Rachel smile. She knew Avery was more of a hands-on kind of guy, not a desk clerk. "If you can get away for a few days, Ariel offered to book a hotel room on the beach for me near her house. That way I can track down some leads. We could also use it as a getaway."

"Ooh, that sounds enticing," he said, his voice husky. "Let me see if I can get away from here. What days were you thinking?"

"It would have to be soon. I thought maybe next Thursday through Sunday."

"I'll check and let you know. It's about time we got together again."

She could practically see his smile from the sexy sound of his voice.

After they'd hung up, Rachel sat at her desk and opened

the file folder Ariel had given her. There were only a few newspaper clippings, so she read through them. All stated that Randall had been out in the Gulf alone when the boat had suddenly blown up. His close friend, Adrian Carlisle, had also been boating in the area and rushed to the scene, but there was nothing to be found. Randall had died in the explosion. A week later, part of a human leg had floated to shore, and DNA determined it was Randall.

Rachel cringed. It was awful thinking about someone being blown to pieces like that. Almost all the reports were the same, except one did give a few more details. The reporter had interviewed Ariel, and she'd said she'd been the person to supply the DNA sample from hair left in a hairbrush that was still at her house. Rachel thought about that a moment. Would a person still have her ex-husband's hairbrush—hair and all—lying around her house months after they'd divorced? Then she remembered that Randall had lived on the boat after moving out of their house. Maybe he'd stored some of his possessions at Ariel's house. But a hairbrush?

Shaking off that thought, Rachel turned to her computer and began searching for more information about Randall's death. There was little online that offered any more information than she'd already read. The lead investigator, Jack Meyers, was quoted in one newspaper saying there was no evidence of terrorism or illegal use of the boat. Randall Weathers had an impeccable reputation, so the explosion was marked down to a fuel leak and faulty engine.

"Can an engine blow up by itself?" Rachel asked aloud. It seemed as though Randall's boat had exploded without any warning. Why did they believe it may have been a gas leak and fire?

Rachel pulled out a sheet of paper to make a list. She had several questions she wanted to ask Jack Meyers. She also wanted to talk to Randall's best friend, Adrian. There seemed like there were too many holes in Randall's death, and she was determined to find answers.

CHAPTER THREE

It turned out Avery couldn't take time off to go to Panama City Beach with Rachel, so she asked her daughter instead. Jules jumped at the chance of a weekend at the beach. She couldn't go on Thursday with her mother but would drive there Friday after classes.

"That will give you a chance to talk to some of the people before I get there," Jules told Rachel. "And then we can have some fun."

Rachel laughed. "You mean like shopping fun?"

"Is there any other type?" her daughter had asked.

Before leaving town, Rachel stopped by the Magnolia Memory Care Center, where her Aunt Julie resided. She wanted to make sure her aunt knew she'd be away for the weekend. But as she entered the building, her spirits dropped as they usually did during her visits. Her aunt had once been a vibrant, busy woman who loved life. Now, Alzheimer's had turned her into a shell of her old self, living inside her own head and barely participating in the world around her. But Rachel always made sure to visit her several times a week, despite her aunt no longer recognizing her.

Rachel knocked at her aunt's apartment door and then entered cautiously. "Aunt Julie? Can I come in? It's Rachel." Because Julie rarely knew who she was these days, Rachel was always careful to announce herself.

Julie was sitting on her sofa, watching a game show on television. Shirley, one of her caretakers, was in the room with her.

"Well, lookie here, Miss Julie," Shirley said in her soft southern drawl. "Rachel has come to visit."

Rachel adored Shirley. She was always so cheerful and caring with her aunt. "Hi, Shirley. How are you today?"

"I'm doing just fine, dear," Shirley said. She walked closer to Rachel, her black curly hair bobbing as she moved. "I'm afraid your aunt isn't as lucid today as she is other days, though," she whispered to Rachel.

Rachel sighed. Since Julie hadn't bothered to look her way when she'd entered, she figured she wasn't having a good day. "Will I upset her if I sit with her a while?" Rachel asked Shirley.

"I don't see what harm it could do," Shirley said. "I'll be right outside the door in the hallway if you need me. I have someone else I need to check on."

Rachel nodded to Shirley as she left and then walked over to the sofa. She sat a short distance away from her aunt so as not to frighten her, but Julie just kept staring at the television.

"I just stopped by to let you know I'll be gone for a few days," Rachel said as if they'd been having a conversation. "Jules is joining me on a trip to Panama City Beach. It'll be fun for the two of us to go away for a few days together."

At the mention of Jules, Julie turned her head and stared at Rachel. "Jules?" she asked.

Rachel smiled. "Yes. Your great-niece, Jules. Actually, she's like a granddaughter to you. Do you remember her?" she asked hopefully.

Julie stared curiously at Rachel a moment and then turned her head back to the television show. Rachel was disappointed. She tried not to expect much from her aunt these days, but sometimes she wished for a miracle.

After a while, Rachel said goodbye to her aunt and quietly left the room. She ran into Shirley in the hallway.

"How'd your visit go?" Shirley asked.

"It was very quiet," Rachel told her sadly. "She seemed to recognize Jules's name but then never said another word. Aunt Julie has declined greatly over the past few weeks."

Shirley nodded. "I'm afraid she has. She doesn't recognize me most of the time, and I see her every day. Her doctor tried a new medication, but so far, it hasn't helped."

"It's so sad," Rachel said, holding back tears that threatened to spill. Her Aunt Julie and Uncle Gordon had raised her like a daughter and treated Jules like their granddaughter. She missed being able to talk to her like they used to.

Rachel told Shirley she'd be away for a few days and not hesitate to call her if anything came up. As she walked to her car, Rachel tried to push away the sadness that had enveloped her during her visit with Julie. There was nothing she could do to help her aunt except give her this nice place to live in and make sure she was cared for. Still, she wished she could do more.

On the two-hour drive to Panama City Beach, Rachel focused on her task ahead. Ariel had generously booked her a hotel room on the beach, just a short walk to the Pier Park Mall. Rachel was looking forward to spending time with Jules and was also excited to investigate Randall's supposed death.

She'd written down a list of places to visit and people she hoped to talk to. The first place on her list was the local police department to speak to the detective who'd covered the case. Then she planned on going to the marina where Randall's boat had been docked and where his best friend lived.

Rachel was genuinely pleased when she checked into her hotel room. As promised, it was directly on the beach with two queen beds and a balcony they could sit on to enjoy the ocean breezes. They were on the third floor, so the view was perfect.

She immediately texted a picture of their room and view to Jules and then to Avery.

"I'll bet you wish you'd come after all," she'd texted to Avery.

"Lol," he texted back. *"The view is beautiful, but I'd be happy being with you anywhere."*

Rachel smiled to herself. She missed Avery and hoped to see him soon. He was kind, intelligent, and incredibly handsome. She couldn't wait until they were able to be together again.

It was two o'clock by the time Rachel was in her car again, driving the short distance to the police station. The weather was warm and sunny, and she'd changed into tan cotton slacks and a lightweight black t-shirt before heading out. The traffic was heavy, and soon she found the station and parked, then walked inside. A female officer sat at the front desk.

"Is it possible to talk to Lieutenant Meyers?" Rachel asked. That was the name on the card that Ariel had given her.

"Just a moment," the officer said, hitting a button on her phone.

A moment later, a tall man in a navy-blue suit walked toward Rachel. "Were you looking for me?" he asked, offering his hand to shake.

"Lieutenant Meyers?" Rachel asked, shaking his hand.

When he nodded, she continued. "I'm Rachel Emery. I was wondering if I could speak to you about the Randall Weathers case."

The officer stared at her a moment as if trying to place her. "May I ask why?"

"His ex-wife, Ariel Weathers, asked me to look into his death. I'm doing this as a favor for a friend." Rachel felt uncomfortable under Lieutenant Meyers's intense stare. His brown hair was cropped short, and his eyes were a deep brown, but there was no denying he was all business as he gave her the once-over.

"Let's go to my office where we can talk privately," he finally said. He motioned for her to go first and then followed her through the office crowded with desks. Pointing to a door on a side wall, she walked inside, and he closed the door. "Can I get you something to drink?" he asked politely.

"No, thank you," Rachel said. She watched as the Lieutenant stepped around to the other side of his desk. Surprisingly, his desktop was very neat, with only a few file folders stacked on one corner.

He motioned for her to sit, and he also did. "What would you like to know about the Weathers's case?" he asked.

"I was wondering if it's possible to get a copy of the official report on the case now that's it's been closed," Rachel said. "I'd like to look through it."

Lieutenant Meyers cocked his head. "Do you think you'll find something we didn't?"

"No, no," Rachel said quickly. "I'm sure you did a thorough job. I'd just like to go over it."

"Are you a private investigator?" he asked.

Rachel laughed. "No. Not at all. Just a friend trying to help."

The Lieutenant frowned but remained quiet. He stood and walked to a file cabinet. "I'm old school. I like keeping paper copies of important cases," he said as he dug through the folders. Finally, he pulled one out of the drawer and turned back to Rachel. "I'm in no way obligated to share this with you, but I don't see any harm in it. If you'll wait here a moment, I'll have someone copy these for you."

"That would be great," she said, relieved. For a moment, she'd thought he wasn't going to give her anything. "Thank you."

Lieutenant Meyers left the office and returned a moment later. He sat down on the edge of his desk. "Can I ask why Mrs. Weathers wants you to look over these files?"

Rachel wished she could tell him the truth, but she knew Ariel wouldn't want her to. The Lieutenant seemed like a nice guy, and she hated lying. "I think she just wants to make sure all was done to identify her husband's remains," she told him. "It must be difficult accepting someone is gone when so little of them is found for identification."

The Lieutenant nodded. "I can understand that. But she seemed more than willing to accept that he'd died a few months ago. She was the one who gave us the hair samples so we could test his DNA." He hesitated a moment, then said, "And she accepted the life insurance money without any question."

Rachel's brows rose. "How do you know that?"

He shrugged. "We keep track of every aspect of a case, even after it's closed."

A uniformed officer came in with two files of papers and handed them to Lieutenant Meyers, then left. The Lieutenant gave one of the files to Rachel.

"It's all in there," he said. "I have nothing to hide. If you learn anything new, I hope you'll give me a call and let me know."

Rachel rose and accepted the file. "Thank you. I appreciate this. Not all law enforcement agencies are so willing to help, believe me."

A broad smile broke out on his face. "Spoken like someone who knows. And very true."

Rachel smiled back. She realized he was not so buttoned-up as he'd first appeared. "Well, thank you, Lieutenant. I appreciate the help."

"Call me Jack, please," he said. "All this Lieutenant stuff is too formal."

"Okay, Jack. Thank you." She turned to leave, and Jack followed her out to the parking lot.

"I hope you find what you're looking for," he said as she walked toward her car.

Rachel turned. "I hope I don't," she said seriously. She hopped into her car and drove off.

* * *

Rachel followed highway 98 back toward Panama City. The Shady Cove Marina wasn't too far away, and she wanted to see where Randall had docked his yacht. After crossing the bridge, she easily found the marina and parked in the lot beside the restaurant. As she walked on the sidewalk around the building, the marina suddenly came into view with the sparkling blue water of the bay. Rachel stopped and took in the picturesque sight. The bay was large, and the water glittered in the afternoon sun. Although she'd never had a fascination with boating, Rachel could see why someone would enjoy being out on the water on a day like today.

Rachel continued walking alongside the restaurant, The Mermaid's Cove, and could smell the delicious aroma of seafood cooking. There was a two-tier deck on the front of the restaurant, facing the marina. A few people sat at tables with umbrellas, sipping colorful drinks. From her conversation with Ariel, Rachel knew that this was the place where Randall had drank his nights away.

Gazing around, she immediately noticed a camera set up on the second-tier deck overlooking the marina. She made a mental note to check if they still had footage from the day Randall took his yacht out to the Gulf.

There were fifteen slips in this private marina. Most of the boats were large, extravagant yachts, but there were a couple that were smaller, older boats. Ariel had told her Randall's slip was number fourteen, and his friend's slip was number thirteen. Rachel wondered if the best friend ever thought the number on his spot was unlucky.

She walked out along the dock toward number fourteen. No boat was tied there. Either it hadn't been rented yet, or the occupants were out on the water on this beautiful day. Stopping in front of the empty slip, Rachel gazed around her, turning in a slow circle. She didn't know what she was looking for—she was only observing everything in view. Rachel noted that one of the older boats across the way and two slips down had a camera attached to a pole on its deck. It was pointed directly at her.

"Are you looking for something?" a male voice asked from behind her.

Rachel jumped and quickly turned around. She was staring into the face of a younger, rather good-looking man. "You scared me," she said, then laughed. "I was just studying the area."

The man ran his hand over his hair even though it was closely cropped. Rachel wondered if he'd recently cut it shorter. He was tall and lean, with curious hazel eyes and a deep tan.

"I'm sorry I scared you," he said in a deep voice. He shoved his hands nervously into the pockets of his cargo shorts. "What were you studying?"

"I was just looking around the area," she said. "Do you own one of these yachts?"

His frown changed into a small smile. "I'd hardly call what I own a yacht, but yes, I own the one right there." He pointed to slip thirteen, where a smaller boat was docked.

Rachel nodded. This had to be Randall's friend, Adrian Carlisle. She offered her hand to shake. "You must be Adrian. I'm Rachel Emery, a friend of Ariel Weathers."

He hesitated a moment as he studied her, then finally shook her hand. "It's nice to meet you," he said cautiously. "I'm sorry, but I'm a little confused. Why would a friend of Ariel's be here?"

Rachel had nothing to hide. "Ariel asked me to do a little investigating into Randall's death. She told me you lived on your boat here, and you were Randall's best friend. I wanted to see the marina and possibly speak with you."

"It's been almost a year since Randall died. The case is closed. Why would she be looking into it now?" His feet shifted nervously.

Rachel glanced around and again noted the camera that was trained on them. "Could we talk somewhere private?"

Adrian glanced to where she was looking, then nodded. He turned toward his boat. "Follow me," he said. Adrian stepped over from the dock onto the back of the boat and then offered his hand to Rachel. "We wouldn't want you to fall into the water," he said with a grin.

Rachel definitely didn't want that to happen. She glanced around the boat. There was a small sitting area with padded cushions and a glass sliding door that led inside the living area. She followed Adrian through the door and down three steps into a combination kitchen/dining room.

"Would you like anything to drink?" he asked, opening the compact refrigerator.

"No, thank you," she said. The room reminded her of being inside an RV.

Adrian pulled out a can of beer for himself and snapped the top open. He waved for her to sit down at the dinette, and he sat also. "So, what can I do for you?"

Rachel felt a little claustrophobic in the small space, but she put a smile on her face. "Ariel told me you live on your boat. How long have you lived here?"

"Oh, about four years. It was either a small house or a boat. I love the water, so I decided I'd buy a boat as my house." He laughed. "Unlike Randall, I couldn't afford both."

"I doubt most people can," Rachel said. "Yachts are expensive, aren't they?"

"Depends on what you buy," Adrian said. "Mine is old and not very big, but I'm fine with it. Randall's yacht, on the other hand, was a beaut. But then, he and Ariel had the money to buy a brand-new yacht."

"When did they buy theirs?" Rachel asked.

Adrian sat back and thought a moment. "I think about five years ago. I know he had his first, and that's how I ended up renting the slip next to his."

"Have you known Randall a long time?"

He chuckled. "Practically all my life. We grew up together and went to the same schools. At least through high school. Randall went on to college, but I went to trade school."

"Really. What do you do for a living?" Rachel asked.

"Well, I went to school to fix heating and cooling units. But I don't do that anymore. I work for a company that takes tourists out on cruises and deep-sea fishing in the Gulf."

"So, you really do like the water," Rachel said, grinning. "It's great you can do what you love."

He nodded, then looked uncomfortable again. "I'm sure this isn't what you wanted to talk about, though."

"Actually, I find this all interesting. But you're right. I wanted to ask you about the day Randall's boat blew up. Ariel said you had followed him out to the Gulf in your boat. Did you see his boat explode?"

He nodded solemnly. "Yes, I did. And I know who's responsible for it catching on fire."

Her brows rose. "Who?"

Adrian looked at her sorrowfully. "Me."

CHAPTER FOUR

"You?" Rachel asked, shocked by his confession. She hadn't read any reports saying that Adrian was responsible for Randall's death.

"Yes." Adrian took a long drink of his beer. "He'd asked me the week before to look at his engine because it kept over-heating. I'd meant to, but I was busy working and never got a chance. He invited me to go with him when he took it out that day, but I declined. Then I felt guilty for letting him go out alone—something no one should do—and I took my boat out to check on him. When his yacht caught fire, I was devastated. It was all my fault." He dropped his head.

"You can't blame yourself," Rachel said soothingly. "If Randall had been worried about the engine, he never would have taken it out that day. It's not your fault."

Adrian lifted his head and looked at her. "He was my friend, but I didn't take a few minutes to do that small favor for him. Because of me, the engine blew up."

She shook her head. "According to the reports I read, it didn't blow up. The police think a fire started and got out of control quickly. Even if you had checked his engine, it might still have happened."

Adrian frowned. "Is that in the official report? That it caught fire? I was there. The boat exploded into a million pieces. There was nothing left. And no one left, either."

Rachel felt terrible for Adrian. He seemed like a nice guy, and he'd been holding on to this guilt for nearly a year. "However it happened, it wasn't your fault. Believe me. It was an accident."

He took another sip of beer and composed himself. "So, what's Ariel looking to find after all this time?"

"I don't think she expects to find anything new. She just wants fresh eyes to look at it, just for her peace of mind. But whatever she's looking for, believe me, she doesn't blame you."

"That's good to hear," Adrian said, looking relieved. "I really liked Randall and Ariel. They were a fun couple. We'd gone on several trips together on their yacht to the Bahamas. It was always a good time."

"Did Randall have a serious girlfriend before his accident?" Rachel asked. "Or do you know if he had trouble with anyone?"

Adrian shook his head. "No to both. He saw women, but not seriously. He hung out at The Mermaid's Cove a lot and had a few parties on his boat. But to tell you the truth, he was still hung up on Ariel. She's a hard woman to forget."

Rachel found his last statement interesting. *A hard woman to forget.* She wondered if Adrian had a crush on Ariel. Pushing that thought aside, she stood. "Thank you for talking to me. I'm sorry you lost your good friend. I know how hard it is to lose someone."

"Thank you," he said. Adrian glanced at the clock on the microwave. "Oh, I'm sorry, but I have to take off. I have an evening shift taking tourists out for a sunset cruise."

They went their separate ways, Rachel staying on the dock near the yacht and Adrian hurrying away to his car. She turned her attention to the camera on the other boat and started walking that way. Just as she reached it, an older man wearing a faded Hawaiian shirt, long shorts, and a fishing hat came up from below and onto the deck. He smiled through his scruffy white beard at Rachel, his dark eyes squinting.

"Did you get anything out of him?" the old man asked in a raspy voice. "He's a slippery one, don't you think?"

Rachel found the older man amusing. He looked like a character out of an old 1950s sea movie. "Why do you think he's slippery?" she asked.

The older man snorted. "That guy knows more than he claims; I'll bet my boat on it." He laughed. "Not that anyone would want this old thing." He nodded at the boat under his feet.

"It looks like you've kept your boat up nicely," Rachel said. She pointed to the camera on the pole. "And you've added some new technology."

The older man looked to where she was pointing. "Ah, yeah. That thing. Well, sometimes a little technology helps to scare away the scallywags." He grinned, then raised his hand to shake. "The name is Rusty. Rusty Garrett," he said.

Rachel couldn't help but smile. The name suited him. "I'm Rachel Emery," she said, reaching to shake his hand. "It's nice to meet you."

"Well, what can I do for you, missy?" Rusty asked. "Pardon my bluntness, but I saw you staring at the camera a few times, and I figured you had something on your mind."

"Oh, well," she was at a loss for words. Rachel hadn't realized he was watching people with the camera from below. "I just noticed you had it and wondered if it was in place the night before Randall Weathers died. Or that same day, too."

"That's what I figured you were wondering," he said, tipping his fishing hat back a bit on his head. "A pretty girl like you wouldn't be hanging around here unless she had a good reason. And when I saw you talking to Adrian, I figured you had a purpose."

She grinned. "Why didn't you think I might be his girlfriend?"

He grunted. "I knew you couldn't be. Let's just say that you're several steps up the ladder from what he usually brings back to his boat."

Rachel's brows rose. "You must see everything that goes on around here."

"Well, I'm not some nosey old housewife, but I do keep track of who's running around my boat. This here's my home as well, and I would like it to be safe."

"Can't blame you for that," Rachel said.

"To answer your question, I've had the camera for over a year, so I did catch all the comings and goings right before Randall's boat exploded. To tell you the truth, I was surprised the police never asked to see my footage. A lot happened that night before he went out on the water. But they didn't seem to care. They asked me a few questions, and that was it."

This intrigued Rachel. "Is that why you put up the camera? Because there was so much activity going on?"

"Yes, that, and because we have a little trouble with transients around here. Now, don't get me wrong. I have no problem with people who are down on their luck, and I've been known to give money now and then to those in need. But some thieving was going on and the damaging of boats around here.

And one morning, I even found a man sleeping on my deck. So, I put up the camera to keep an eye on my boat while I'm below."

Rachel nodded. "That was smart."

Rusty pointed to his head. "Yep. I do have a little something up here between my ears." He laughed. "But there were also the parties going on over at slip fourteen. Once Randall started living on his yacht, there seemed to be parties and noise there all the time. I wanted to keep track of who was coming and going around here."

Rachel found that interesting. "Do you keep footage stored from your camera?"

He winked at her. "You bet I do. Tell me the dates you want, missy, and I can put it on one of those little thumb drives for you."

"That would be great," she said, delighted she'd talked to Rusty. He was a little rough around the edges, just as his boat was, but he was a goldmine of information. She told him the timeline she would like to see, and he nodded.

"If you can drop by tomorrow, I'll have it ready for you," he said. Then Rusty cocked his head and stared at her. "Are you one of those private investigators or something?"

She laughed. "No. Not professionally. A friend of mine asked me to look into Randall's death. So, any new leads would be helpful."

"Well, then, I'll see you tomorrow, young lady." He tipped his hat and headed back down below.

"Interesting character," a male voice said directly behind Rachel.

She spun and found herself looking into the brown eyes of Lieutenant Jack Meyers.

* * *

"Are you following me?" Rachel asked, indignant.

"Yes, I believe I am." He grinned, then nodded toward the restaurant. "Can I buy you dinner? I'm starved."

"What?"

"I'm sorry I startled you," Jack said. "I didn't mean to. Let's get a bite to eat, and we can talk."

"Fine," Rachel said, still incensed he'd been following her. She stormed past him and led the way.

Once inside and seated, Rachel got to the point. "Why are you following me?" She watched as Jack slowly unfolded his napkin and placed it in his lap. *Arrogant,* she thought.

"When I met you at the station earlier, I thought you looked familiar. Then, it hit me. You're Rachel Parnell, the woman whose body was supposed to be in the little girl's grave in California. I remembered your face being plastered all over the news for several weeks. So, that piqued my interest. Why would Rachel Parnell be digging into Randall Weathers's murder?"

Rachel rolled her eyes. "My name is Rachel Emery. And yes, I was the woman who helped solve the case of my supposed death as a child. But that has nothing to do with Randall's death."

"Then why the interest? You're not a writer, are you? Like Ariel Weathers."

She shook her head. "No. I actually design book covers for a living. I don't write books. But I'm friends with Ariel, and she thought since I was able to help solve my own case, I might be able to help her."

"Help her with what?" Jack asked, his brow creasing.

The waitress came and took their drink and food order. Rachel only ordered a salad and a Coke, while Jack ordered a whole shrimp and steak dinner. Rachel studied him as he spoke to the waitress. He was very polite and well-spoken. He also looked professional in his dark suit. Jack Meyers was no slouch. He seemed like a guy who worked out daily and took care of himself. No donuts or junk food for him.

Jack cleared his throat, and Rachel was shaken out of her thoughts. "You were saying?" he said.

Rachel replied testily. "As I said earlier today, Ariel feels that some things may have been overlooked. She wants to be sure the body part found truly was her ex-husband's."

"The DNA sample she supplied matched, so why wouldn't it be Randall's?" he asked.

He was right, of course. Rachel couldn't argue with that point, so she changed the subject. "Am I doing anything illegal by investigating this case? After all, your department closed it."

Jack sat back in his seat, and a slow smile spread across his face. "No. You aren't doing anything illegal. I'm just curious."

Their drinks came, and the waitress left.

Jack continued. "Can I be completely candid with you?"

"Yes. I'd prefer that," Rachel said, relieved.

"That case never sat well with me. It was so odd. An expensive yacht like that just blowing up in the Gulf. And then only his leg floated to shore. And the fact that his best friend just happened to witness the explosion while on his own boat. It was all so tidy."

Rachel frowned. She'd had a few reservations, too, but knowing the lead investigator had them was interesting. "What do you mean by tidy?"

"Just between you and me," he said. "All the boxes were checked. His boat exploded. A witness who happened to know him saw it. The wife supplied the DNA sample for the ex-husband. The one leg floating to shore. Why didn't his arm or even head float to shore? Why something that couldn't be identified by dental records or fingerprints?"

Rachel grimaced at the thought of a head floating to shore and someone finding it. With this thought in mind, their food was served. She no longer had an appetite, but Jack dug right in.

"Sorry about being so graphic, but you get the point, right? The only body parts that couldn't be identified without the help of a friend or family member are the torso or legs. How convenient his leg washed up." Jack forked a shrimp and placed it in his mouth.

"I get what you're saying," Rachel said, picking at her salad. "But you accepted the conclusion and closed the case."

He shrugged. "I had no choice. We don't have the manpower to keep a case open that has been so tidily summed up. But then you came into the office, and that set off my radar. Now, I'm interested again."

Rachel couldn't blame him. She'd be just as curious if she were him. But she also couldn't tell him that Ariel was seeing her dead ex-husband everywhere, and it was scaring her to death.

"Have you read the case file yet?" he asked, slicing into his steak.

"No. I was going to go over it tonight. I just wanted to get a feel for the marina first."

"Well, it might help to read the file. And if you have any questions, feel free to call me," Jack said.

"Thank you. I will."

"Oh. And don't bother asking this restaurant for footage from their camera the night before his boat exploded. We did, and for some reason, their camera wasn't 'working.'" He used air quotes to emphasize the last word.

"You don't believe them?" Rachel asked.

"Let's just say that Randall and the owner were quite chummy. If there was anything incriminating on that video, it was erased."

"What do you think might have been on there? Other than the fact that there was a party on the boat the night before he went out on the water," Rachel said.

Jack raised his eyes to Rachel's. "What party? Where did you hear that?"

She was surprised he hadn't known. "Rusty Garrett told me. The older guy you called a character."

Jack shook his head. "See now. I've never heard that before. Seems to me his friend Adrian or someone here at the restaurant would have told me that."

"Do you think it means anything?" she asked.

"It could. Knowing who was on that boat the night before could pinpoint who sabotaged the engine."

Rachel frowned. "I thought the official conclusion was the boat caught on fire, then the gas tank exploded. Wasn't it just an accident?"

Jack looked both ways to see if anyone was listening, then he moved closer to Rachel. "That was what they speculated had happened," he said quietly. "But we've always suspected there was more to it. Either someone else or Randall sabotaged that engine. I just can't figure out who or why."

"It couldn't have been Randall. Why would he want to die in an explosion?" Rachel asked.

"Well, that's the two-million-dollar question, isn't it?"

"What is?" Rachel was confused.

"Whether or not Randall Weathers actually died."

CHAPTER FIVE

Rachel stared at Jack in disbelief. Did he know Randall hadn't died in the explosion? Then why would he have closed the case?

Jack chuckled. "Or at least the one-million-dollar question," he said. "After all, that's what his half of the life insurance money would have been."

"You're just speculating. You don't know anything for certain, do you?" Rachel asked, relaxing again.

Jack shook his head. "No. But it wouldn't surprise me if he faked his death and his wife was in on it. I'm sorry. I know she's a friend of yours. But couples do it all the time and then leave quietly and end up in some foreign country, living off the insurance money."

Rachel thought about the Bahama house Ariel was buying. Was that what they were doing? But why would Ariel bring her into the mix to investigate Randall's death? That would be stupid, and Ariel was anything but stupid.

As they finished their meal, Jack asked Rachel about the case of her supposed death thirty-five years ago, and she told him a little about it. He seemed fascinated by her story.

"I can see why Ariel Weathers hired you to look into her ex-husband's case. You seem to pick up on details others miss," he said, clearly impressed.

"It was nothing," Rachel said quickly. "It was mostly my stubbornness that helped solve the case."

"Don't do that," Jack said seriously. "Don't sell yourself short. You obviously have a sharp mind, so take the compliment with pride."

She was surprised by his stern tone but understood what he meant. She often brushed away compliments because they made her uncomfortable. "Thank you," she said.

He smiled. "You're welcome."

Jack insisted on paying for the meal, and they walked out to their cars as the sun was setting.

"I hope I hear from you again," Jack said. "I meant it when I said I'd be interested in anything new you dig up."

"I'll stay in touch," she told him. Rachel liked how he took his work seriously. "I'm staying over the weekend at a hotel, so if I find anything out, I'll let you know."

"Here." Jack pulled one of his cards out of his jacket pocket. He wrote something on the back, then handed it to her. "My cell number, in case I'm not at the office."

Rachel's brows rose. "Won't Mrs. Meyers be upset if you get calls at home on the weekend?"

He laughed. "No. There's no Mrs. Meyers. Just me and my dog, Captain. And he isn't the clingy type."

She chuckled. "Let me guess. You have a German Shepherd."

"That's police profiling." He smiled wide. "And yeah, you're right."

She waved goodbye and turned to get into her car as he walked away. Rachel looked over the marina one last time, watching the beautiful orange sunset over the water. It was then that she saw Adrian walking down the dock to his boat. She glanced at her watch. It was only six o'clock. Hadn't he said he was taking tourists out for an evening cruise on the Gulf?

She wondered why he would lie about something like that. Maybe tomorrow, after she stopped at Rusty's boat for the thumb drive, she'd get a chance to see Adrian again.

Rachel drove the short distance back to her hotel and settled in for the night. Leaving the patio window open to hear the gentle ocean waves, Rachel changed into comfy sweats and lay down on the bed to read the police file.

As she read the report, Rachel realized she wasn't learning anything that she hadn't already read in the newspaper accounts. The police had looked into any connection to drug or human smuggling as a motive to sabotage the yacht, but no ties to nefarious acts had been found. As far as the police could determine, Randall was simply out on his yacht for a leisurely cruise on the Gulf when the engine caught on fire, and the gas tank exploded. As far as witnesses knew, he was alone on the boat. It was just an odd accident.

Jack was right. It all seemed quite tidy.

While reading Adrian's interview, Rachel was surprised he hadn't mentioned Randall had a boat party the night before he died. In fact, he said very little except for feeling guilty about not going out with Randall on his yacht and following him on his own boat after his friend had left. It was pretty much the same story he'd told Rachel. Word for word.

Her phone buzzed around ten o'clock, and she smiled when she saw it was Avery. "Well, hello there. Are you regretting not being here with me this weekend?" she teased.

"I regret not being with you every weekend," he said huskily.

"How was your day of sleuthing?"

She told him what she'd learned and about having dinner with Jack Meyers.

"Wait. What? You're already replacing me with a mere Lieutenant?" he said in mock jealousy.

"Never," she told him. "Now that I have read most of the police report on Randall's death, I understand why Jack thinks the case is too tidy. And why he was following me. But don't worry. He'll never outrank my FBI guy." She giggled.

"Phew! I was afraid I'd have to rush down there and fight for you. My fighting skills aren't up to snuff right now. But seriously, it sounds like you've already learned some things that someone wanted to keep hidden. Like the party the night before his death. Be careful who you trust, okay?"

"Absolutely," she agreed.

"Changing the subject, I managed to get off for four days over Thanksgiving next weekend. Are you sure you still want me to come?"

"Are you kidding? Of course, I want you to come. I haven't seen you in weeks." Rachel was ecstatic. She and Avery were finally going to be together again. "And I can finally introduce you to Jules. She can't wait to meet you."

"I can't wait to meet her, too. But mostly, I can't wait to see you," Avery said. He gave her his flight information for Wednesday night. He was flying directly into Tallahassee.

"By the way, I looked into Randall Weathers's past, and it came up completely clean. Not even a parking ticket. That guy was as pure as the driven snow," Avery said.

"I doubt anyone is that clean," Rachel said. "Thanks for looking him up, though. Maybe all this was just a weird accident, and maybe Ariel is hallucinating. I mean, she might feel guilty about getting all that money for his death, and it's making her see things."

"Maybe," Avery said, sounding cautious. "But you saw the guy on the surveillance tape. So, someone is messing with her. Maybe not her dead ex, though."

"Yeah. I'd wondered about that too. It could be someone impersonating him. But why?" Rachel asked.

"Well, I can think of two million reasons why," Avery teased.

Rachel agreed. It wasn't altogether impossible that someone was trying to scare her out of her money.

They talked a while longer, and then Rachel yawned. "I think it's time for bed. I have another long day tomorrow, talking to people who knew Randall, and then Jules will be here."

"Okay. Have a great time with your daughter. Just don't fall in love with Lieutenant Jack before I come next weekend, okay?" Avery said.

She chuckled. "Never."

They hung up, and Rachel lay back on the bed. She loved how she and Avery could talk so easily with each other. She'd missed that type of close relationship since her husband died. She couldn't wait to see Avery next weekend. It had been too long.

Her phone buzzed, and she smiled, thinking it was Avery again. She was surprised when she saw it was a call from Ariel.

"Hello?" Rachel said.

"He's here again," Ariel whispered into the phone. "I'm all alone, and he's right at the back door. I'm afraid he might kill me!"

* * *

Rachel heard the fear in Ariel's voice. "Call the police. You can't be alone with him out there," she told her.

"I can't," Ariel whimpered. "Please come over. I'm scared." The phone clicked off.

Rachel was terrified for Ariel. Her heart pounding, she quickly changed into jeans and tennis shoes, then rushed out the door to her car. On the way to Ariel's house, she called Jack Meyer's cell phone. "Ariel's in danger. Can you meet me at her house?"

"Let me send a patrol car," Jack said.

"No! This can't be radioed all over for everyone to hear. Please, can you come? I'm heading there right now."

"I'm out the door," Jack said.

Rachel arrived before Jack and flew out of her car and up to Ariel's front door. All the lights were off in the house, and a shiver ran up her spine. What if Randall, or whoever was impersonating him, had already hurt Ariel?

The door opened before Rachel could knock, and someone grabbed her wrist and pulled her inside, shutting the door behind them. Fear gripped Rachel. A flashlight popped on, and there was Ariel's face in the yellow light.

"Oh, my God! You scared me to death," Rachel whispered. She glanced around. "Is he still here?"

Ariel nodded and motioned for Rachel to follow her toward the back patio door. The only light in the yard was from the pool, but Rachel saw him immediately. He was standing only a few feet away, staring directly at them.

Ariel quickly pulled Rachel back around a corner. "I'm so scared," she said, her voice shaking. "What if he tries to get in?"

Rachel agreed it was creepy. He was just standing there, staring. She peered around the corner to see if she could get a good look at the man. He was mostly in shadow, but his height and the cut of his hair looked very much like Randall's.

"What if you turn all the outside lights on at once?" Rachel whispered. "Do you think it would scare him away?"

"I don't know. I'm scared to death to see for sure if it's really Randall. He's supposed to be dead," Ariel said in a shaky voice.

Rachel's phone buzzed, and she looked at it.

"I'm at the front door," Jack had texted.

Rachel hurried to the door with Ariel right behind her. "What's going on?" Ariel asked, looking confused.

Rachel opened the door and whispered to Jack, "He's in the backyard. Hurry!"

Ariel's eyes widened. "What is he doing here? I said not to involve the police."

Rachel ignored Ariel as she watched Jack pull out his gun and head for the back door. She knew he saw the shadow of a man immediately, backlit from the pool light. Jack stopped and stared at Rachel.

"Who is it?" he asked quietly.

"Randall," Rachel said.

In the dark, Rachel couldn't tell what Jack's expression was, but she was sure he was stunned. She watched as he moved stealthily to the patio door and quietly slide it open. He pointed his gun toward the shadowy man and yelled, "Police! Hold it right there!"

Ariel grabbed Rachel's arm. "Why is he here? He'll ruin everything!"

"He's here to help," Rachel said sternly. It baffled her why Ariel wouldn't want help from the police. She turned toward the backyard and watched as the shadow man fled. He climbed effortlessly over the stone wall into the neighbor's yard. Jack didn't follow him. He holstered his pistol and walked back into the house.

"It's safe. He's gone," Jack said. "Can we get some lights on in here?"

Ariel walked around, snapping on lights. From her demeanor, Rachel could tell she was not pleased. The three of them stood in the kitchen, which no longer looked terrifying.

"Now, can someone explain to me why you think the man in the yard was Randall?" Jack asked, his hands on his hips.

"I have no idea who that was," Ariel said haughtily as she floated around the kitchen. She was wearing magenta-colored satin lounge pajamas and a flowing flowery robe. "All I know is a man showed up in my yard and scared the bejesus out of me."

"Why did you call Rachel instead of the police?" Jack asked. He was in jeans and a sweatshirt, but he sounded as professional as if he were wearing his suit.

"I don't know," Ariel said. "I panicked. I didn't know who to call."

"Well, nine-one-one might have been the right choice," Jack quipped.

"I was frantic!" Ariel said, waving her arms around. "Who can think straight when they're upset?"

"Ariel, stop the theatrics, please," Jack said sternly. "I heard you tell Rachel that my being here will 'ruin everything.' What did that mean?"

Ariel stopped moving around and stared straight at Jack. Somehow, she'd managed to squeeze tears from her eyes. "I was afraid to call the police," she said, sounding defeated. "You know how the press gets all over these things. If anyone heard that I'm seeing my dead ex-husband around the house, they'll drag me through the mud and ruin my writing career. And that's all I have left." She grabbed a tissue from a box on the counter and dabbed at her eyes.

Rachel watched her with interest. Ariel really knew how to play a part when she needed to. She glanced at Jack and could tell he wasn't buying any of it.

"If anyone comes near your house again, please call the police. Or call me," he told Ariel. "You have no idea what that man's intentions are."

Ariel nodded. She turned to Rachel, continuing with the dramatics. "I'm so sorry I bothered you, dear. I just didn't know who to turn to. My sister wasn't home, and I just couldn't call the police. You understand, dear, don't you?"

Rachel patted her arm. "I understand. You must have been frightened out of your mind."

"I was," Ariel said, dabbing at her eyes.

"Maybe you should stay the night at the hotel where Rachel is staying," Jack suggested. "Just in case that man returns."

"Oh, I couldn't," Ariel said. "I'll be fine. I'll lock the doors and make sure the cameras are on. And Alivia should be here any moment. I'll have her sleep in the house tonight instead of the guesthouse."

She nearly pushed them out the door after that, which seemed strange to Rachel. If she really felt her life was in danger, wouldn't Ariel be hesitant to be alone?

Jack walked Rachel to her car. "What the hell was that all about?" he asked quietly so Ariel couldn't hear. "Is she looney?"

Rachel held back a smile. She'd thought the same thing. "She believes Randall is still alive and is trying to get the insurance money from her," she told him.

"What? Do you mean she thinks Randall faked his death?" Jack asked.

Rachel shrugged. "Even you said it all looks too tidy. And after reading the official reports, I have to agree with you on that."

"But where does she fit into all of this?" he asked, nodding toward Ariel's house. "Is she in on it?"

"If she were, would she have called me to help her tonight?"

"I don't know," Jack said, shaking his head. "But she was putting on an act in there. And she couldn't wait to get us out the door. It's suspicious."

"It's weird, I'll give you that. Sorry to have bothered you," Rachel said. "But I didn't feel safe coming here with an intruder on the prowl."

He smiled for the first time that night. "No need to apologize. I was happy to do it. I just don't understand yet what it's all about." He glanced at the house again, then back at Rachel. "Maybe we could have lunch or dinner tomorrow and discuss this some more?"

His invitation took Rachel by surprise. "I'm afraid I can't," she said. "I have a few more people to talk to, and then my daughter is coming for the weekend.

"Oh. Right. So, your husband isn't joining you two?" he asked.

"No. My husband passed away a few years ago. It's just my daughter and me."

"I'm sorry," he said, sounding genuine. "Anyway, call me if any more of this craziness happens. There's some real danger going on here. I'd hate to see you get hurt while helping that lunatic in there."

Rachel laughed. "She's not crazy, I think." She promised to call him if anything else came up, and they went their separate ways. Rachel was only too happy to crawl into bed after all of the night's events.

CHAPTER SIX

Rachel was up early the following day and indulged herself with a long walk on the beach before showering and heading out. There was nothing in the police report about anyone visiting Randall's workplace and talking to his employer. Rachel wasn't sure what she would learn there, but it seemed like it was worth a shot.

She drove across the bridge and south into Panama City where the Unified Investment Corporation was located. Parking in front of a newer, five-story building with large glass windows, Rachel walked inside and glanced around. She found a list of businesses on the wall and took the elevator up to the third floor, where she found the offices. Walking inside, a woman at the front desk asked if she had an appointment.

"I'm not sure who I should speak to," Rachel said, suddenly feeling self-conscious about not having a good reason for being there. "I was hoping to speak with someone who worked with Randall Weathers."

The woman stared at her a moment but quickly composed herself. "Just a minute, please," she said, then dialed a number and spoke quietly to the person on the other line.

Rachel glanced around as she waited. The area she was in was blocked off from the inner offices by a wall with glass doors on either side of it. There were leather chairs for clients to wait in, and the name of the business was written in bronze letters behind the receptionist's desk. It looked like a very refined business.

"Mr. Tisdale will see you," the receptionist said. Rachel looked up in time to see a tall, lanky man with dark, slicked-back hair enter. He raised his hand to shake.

"I'm Roger Tisdale," he said.

Rachel shook his hand. "Rachel Emery. Thank you for seeing me on such short notice. I'd like to speak with you about Randall Weathers."

"Yes. Well," Tisdale paused. "We can talk privately in my office." He turned and led the way to the inner sanctum. There were private offices all around with receptionists at desks in front of each of them. It was quiet, except for the piped-in music coming from above. Mr. Tisdale led her to an office on the left and closed the glass door behind him.

Rachel gazed out the floor-to-ceiling window behind Mr. Tisdale's desk. It had an amazing view of the city. Glancing around the room, she was impressed. Everything in the office looked expensive, from his mahogany desk to the leather chairs.

"Please, make yourself comfortable," Tisdale said. "Can I offer you something to drink?"

"Oh, no, thank you." Rachel sat in one of the cushy leather chairs. "I don't want to take up too much of your time. I'm investigating Randall Weathers's death, and I just wanted to ask a few questions." She thought she saw Tisdale wince at Randall's name.

"Randall worked here for nearly ten years, and I was his

superior for five of those years. I'm not sure what I can tell you. He left his position about four months before his death."

This was news to Rachel. All the reports had said he was employed here at the time of his death. "Oh. I was led to believe he was still working here when he died."

"Yes, well, it was reported that way. I saw no need in refuting it."

"Can I ask why?" Rachel asked.

He studied her a moment, then asked, "Are you a private investigator?"

She smiled and shook her head. "No, I'm not. I'm just looking into his death for his wife, Ariel Weathers. Well, his ex-wife. She feels she never had the whole story."

Tisdale pursed his lips. "Hmph. It wouldn't surprise me that she knows exactly what happened."

His harsh words piqued Rachel's interest. "Anything you can tell me would be helpful," she said.

Tisdale sat very still as if pondering whether to tell her something important. Finally, he asked, "Are you going to report this conversation to the news or the police?"

"No. I'm not here to create a scandal. And I'm not connected with the police. I'm just curious about the days leading up to Randall's death."

Tisdale nodded. "Okay. I guess it doesn't matter now that he's dead. Randall was an exemplary employee for the entire time he worked here—at least, that's what we all believed. He was in line for a promotion, but that all went away when I learned that he'd embezzled money from his clients."

Rachel's eyes grew wide. "Embezzled?"

"Yes. And it was a lot of money. Nearly half a million dollars."

"My goodness," Rachel said. "I had no idea."

"That's because it was never reported. He'd taken the money slowly from accounts over the last two years of his employment. A simple accounting error clued us in when an audit was done on one of his accounts. Then we went through all of his accounts and found he'd siphoned money from several of them."

"Why wasn't he prosecuted?" she asked.

Tisdale took a deep breath and let it out slowly. "Our company couldn't afford the bad press. If clients learned of that kind of breach of trust, they'd leave in droves. And Randall knew that. He walked away with five-hundred-thousand dollars and didn't even have to pay it back. We replaced the money from our own funds."

Rachel couldn't help but think that the stolen money was the perfect motive for murder. "Where do you think that money went after he died?"

"Your guess is as good as mine. It wouldn't surprise me if his wife got it. They may have been divorced, but they were still chummy. Real chummy. He mentioned more than once before he was fired that Ariel spent a lot of time with him on that yacht of his." Tisdale frowned. "Come to think of it, he may have paid off the yacht with the money he stole. I know things were tight for them for a while. He was completely over-extended when he bought that monstrosity."

"Was his yacht expensive?" Rachel asked, unaware of how much one would cost.

Tisdale laughed. "Expensive? Oh, yes, it was. He bought the Cadillac of yachts—a thirty-four-foot Carver C34 Coupe. Those boats can cost upwards of three to five-hundred thousand dollars."

Rachel pondered this new information. Hadn't Ariel said she'd received an insurance check for the value of the boat? So, in truth, she did end up with the stolen money.

"Please do not repeat this to anyone," Tisdale said, suddenly looking nervous. "It could still ruin our business."

"I won't tell anyone," she promised. Rachel stood. "Thank you for clearing a few things up for me. I really doubt that Ariel knew her ex-husband had lost his job. She never mentioned it."

"Well, I hate to be a jerk, but Randall got what was coming to him," Tisdale said.

"I didn't know him personally," Rachel said. "So, I can't say he deserved to die."

"I'm sorry if that sounded harsh, but after what he put this company and me through, there were no tears for him here."

She thanked him again and left the office. All the new information was spinning in her head. Could someone at the office have sabotaged his yacht for revenge? It seemed likely. Rachel hopped into her car and turned back north toward the marina.

By the time she arrived at the marina, Rachel had played all types of scenarios in her mind. Had Randall faked his death? Maybe he was worried about the investment company coming after him. Or maybe he wanted a clean slate and the half a million dollars back, plus the two million from his life insurance. But if that were the case, it would mean that Ariel was involved. Rachel pondered that a while too. Why would Ariel ask her to investigate if she was involved in the whole scheme? That didn't make sense. Yet the night before, Ariel had been irritated that Rachel had involved Jack in the intruder incident. Why didn't she want the police involved if she was afraid for her life? That made her look guilty.

As Rachel parked at the marina, she had to shake all those thoughts out of her head. It was an endless circle of insanity. None of it made sense.

The day was beautiful in the mid-seventies, with the sun shining brightly. She walked down the dock toward Rusty's boat, thinking about her daughter and the fun they'd have together this weekend. With a full college schedule, Jules's busy life made it hard for them to get together often. During her freshman year, they'd been able to meet every week for dinner, but this year she was even busier. Relaxing near the beach and doing some shopping together was exactly what they both needed.

Rusty popped his head out of his quarters as she came into the camera's view. "Hello, pretty lady," he said. "I've been waiting for you. I found something interesting on the video."

Rachel drew nearer. "Really? What?"

"Would you mind coming aboard, and I'll show you on my computer. Wait a moment, and I'll bring it up." Rusty disappeared below deck again as Rachel stepped aboard his boat.

"Come. Sit down here," Rusty said, waving her over to a padded bench.

He was wearing a different Hawaiian shirt today and another pair of faded cargo shorts. With the gray beard and grizzled look about him, he reminded her a little of Ernest Hemingway.

Rachel sat and stared at the laptop screen. The video on it was paused.

"I was going over this video carefully last night to see if there was anything strange," Rusty said. "I'd forgotten just how crazy that party was. Everyone who came down from The Mermaid's Cove was already pretty toasted up."

He played the video as Rachel watched. Several men in beach wear and scantily clothed young women passed by the camera, most of them carrying bottles of wine or beer, all of them unsteady on their feet. There must have been at least twenty-five of them, hooting and hollering as they stepped onto Randall's deck. Randell stood on the edge, looking quite sober, waving the people toward the yacht and helping the ladies on. Rachel recognized one of the men. Adrian stepped onto the boat, swaying on his feet, his arm around a young woman.

"So, Adrian was on the boat that night," Rachel said as Rusty paused the video. "He never mentioned the party to the police or to me."

Rusty nodded. "Seems like a silly thing to keep secret, doesn't it? But that's not all. Watch this." He hit play again, and Rachel watched as a straggler walked behind the group. Randall waved for him to join them, and the man's face lit up. His clothes were ragged, and his hair looked unkempt. He carried a backpack, which was quite dirty. But Randall treated him like an old friend as he stepped onto the yacht.

"Remember when I said I put up the camera because I'd found a homeless man sleeping on my deck?" Rusty asked her.

She nodded.

He pointed to the paused video. "That's the guy. And ever since Randall's death, I haven't seen him hanging around here at night anymore."

Rachel frowned. "What are you saying?"

Rusty shrugged. "I don't know. All I know is that snobby Randall Weathers invited a homeless man to come to his party, and then Randall died the next day. I don't know about you, but that sure seems odd to me."

"You're not blaming the homeless man, are you?" Rachel asked, surprised by this new turn of events.

"Absolutely not. He was just a guy down on his luck. But it seems to me if you'd like some spare body parts floating around while you swim away, a homeless person would be perfect. No one would miss him."

"I hadn't thought of that," Rachel said, pondering this new information.

Rusty fast-forwarded to the end of the video on the thumb drive and pointed out something else. "I was looking over yesterday's video too, and I thought you might find this interesting, so I made a copy for you." He ran the video of a man with longish light hair dressed in dark clothing walking down the dock. He glanced around before stepping onto Adrian's boat and going below.

Rachel watched with interest. "That couldn't have been Adrian. His hair is short and dark."

"My thoughts exactly," Rusty said. "This was around eleven-thirty last night."

Rachel looked directly at Rusty, and he returned her gaze. "Who does he look like to you?" she asked.

Rusty grinned. "It looked exactly like the person you think it looked like. Randall Weathers."

* * *

Rachel left Rusty's boat a while later after thanking him for the copy of the videos. She glanced over at Adrian's boat and wondered if he were home. Her mind was spinning. She'd seen Adrian come back to his boat at sunset yesterday, even though he'd said he had to be at work for an evening cruise. Ariel had called her about ten-fifteen, and the whole intruder episode was over by eleven. That would have given Randall—or whoever was impersonating him—enough time to return to the marina and be seen on the video. But the big question was whether Randall was alive and living on Adrian's boat or if Adrian was impersonating Randall.

Slowly, she walked toward Adrian's boat to see if he was around. As she drew to the edge of the dock, she didn't see him. Turning, she noticed that Rusty's camera was still facing toward her, so she felt safe.

"Adrian?" she called. "Adrian? Are you here?" There was no answer. She thought about yesterday and how Adrian hadn't hesitated to let her into his kitchen area. If he were hiding Randall, wouldn't he have kept her away from the interior? But then, who was the man who stepped onto Adrian's boat last night? Drawing all her courage, Rachel tentatively stepped onto the back deck of the boat.

"Adrian? Are you here?" she called again, moving to the sliding glass door she'd entered yesterday. When there was no answer, she glanced around, then gently pulled on the door's handle. It was unlocked and slid open easily. Her heart pounding in her chest, Rachel forced herself to walk inside, still calling out Adrian's name. Breaking and entering into someone's house was not something she ever thought she'd do. But she had to see if there was any sign of Randall living on the boat.

When no one answered her down below, she slowly walked around the compact area. Beyond the kitchen was a small living room, but you had to duck your head to walk around it. She noticed a shelf with a stereo system, a few CDs, and two framed photos. Rachel moved closer to the pictures and studied them. One was of Adrian and Randall on the deck of a ship with the aqua-blue water of the Caribbean behind them. Adrian's hair was much longer in the photo than it was now. Another was of Adrian and Ariel. He wore only swim shorts, and she was in a bikini. Rachel studied that photo and saw that Alivia sat in the background, also wearing a swimsuit. Alivia was staring at the couple with a creased forehead. She looked angry. Or jealous.

Rachel wondered if Alivia had a crush on Adrian while he had one on Ariel. That would have been a mess. But it wouldn't have had anything to do with murdering Randall.

To the right was another door, which Rachel thought might be the bedroom. One last time, she called out Adrian's name, but there was no response. Walking to the door, she was just about to reach for the handle when a voice came from behind her.

"What are you doing here?"

CHAPTER SEVEN

Rachel jumped and nearly hit her head on the ceiling. She turned, and there stood Adrian. "Oh, my goodness. You scared me again," she said, placing a hand over her thumping heart.

"Why are you down here?" Adrian asked, glaring at her.

"I'm so sorry. I was looking for you. I called your name several times," Rachel said, trying to sound calmer than she felt. She felt so stupid to have thought she wouldn't get caught snooping.

"So, you just walked inside my private quarters?" he asked. He wasn't the nice, quiet guy from yesterday. Adrian was furious, and Rachel couldn't blame him.

"I'm so sorry," Rachel said. She grasped for a reason to be inside his boat. "I was worried about you, so I came in to check. The door was unlocked."

"Worried about me?" he frowned. "Why?"

"Can we go outside for this conversation?" Rachel asked. "I'm feeling a bit claustrophobic down here." He was blocking her way out, and she was becoming increasingly frightened to be down here alone with him.

Adrian ran his hand over his short hair. "Yeah. Okay," he said, sounding a little calmer. He moved aside and let her squeeze past to go above deck.

Once outside, Rachel took a deep breath of ocean air. It cleared her head, and she felt safer.

"Now tell me why you were afraid for me?" Adrian demanded.

"Well, I was talking to Rusty, and he said he saw a strange man get on your boat late last night. Rusty mentioned there has been a little trouble around here with transients, so I thought I should check on you." The lie came easily, which also scared Rachel. She prided herself on being honest.

"Hm. Rusty. He's such a busybody. He shouldn't have scared you like that. I came home late last night. I had that sunset cruise like I told you, then I went out for a few drinks. That old coot needs to have his eyesight checked."

Rachel knew for sure that Adrian had come back to the boat at sunset, so he was lying. But she wasn't in any position to accuse him of that. "Well. That explains it. I'm so sorry I went inside your boat. I promise I won't bother you anymore." She stepped over toward the dock, ready to climb out, but Adrian grabbed her wrist. Rachel turned to look at him.

"Let me help you," he said, no longer looking angry. He held her wrist until she was safely on the dock.

"Thank you," Rachel said, trying to calm her breathing.

"Maybe you'd like to go for a ride out on the Gulf sometime," Adrian said. "I'd be happy to take you."

Yeah, and throw me overboard, Rachel thought. "That would be fun. Thank you for the invitation."

He nodded and headed below deck. Rachel scurried away as fast as she could, back to her car.

* * *

"Oh, my goodness, Mom!" Jules exclaimed as tears of laughter streamed down her cheeks. "I can't believe you actually broke into someone's house and got caught."

Rachel couldn't help but laugh along. It was insane to think about what she'd done that afternoon. "Well, I didn't actually break in—the door was unlocked." This only made her daughter laugh harder.

"Yeah. That makes it so much better," Jules said.

"Well, never again! It scared me half to death when Adrian caught me. I'm not cut out to be a cat burglar," Rachel said, sobering up. This only made her daughter laugh more.

They were sitting on the patio of a Mexican restaurant at Pier Park, finishing their dinner. Jules had arrived at the hotel by five o'clock that afternoon, and they'd gone for a quick walk on the beach before driving the short distance here.

"Do you think Adrian is part of the conspiracy?" Jules asked, growing serious.

"He was definitely mad I was snooping. But then, who wouldn't be? And the first day I met him, he said something strange about Ariel. He said she was a hard woman to forget. I got the feeling that he had a thing for her."

"Hm." Jules sat back and crossed her legs. She was wearing a short skirt that showed off her long legs. "So maybe he killed his best friend to get the wife?"

Rachel shrugged. "There's a long list of suspects. The more people I talk to about Randall, the more suspects I find. I suppose Ariel could have wanted him dead for the money. His boss definitely would have liked to have killed him. Or Randall could have faked his death, and both Adrian and Ariel are in on it. After that stunt she pulled last night, I'm questioning if she's just playing a game with me."

"That's the part that doesn't make sense," Jules said. "Why bring you into it? The police and insurance company believed Randall was dead, and she got her money. He also walked away with the half a million dollars that he'd embezzled. Why ask you to dredge it all up?"

Rachel sipped the last of her margarita. "That's the one thing that makes me rethink everything. Maybe Randall did fake his death, and Ariel didn't know he had. Now he's out to get the money back from her. Adrian could be helping him. It's all very strange."

The two women left the restaurant and walked along the shopping mall back to Rachel's car. The stores were closing for the night, but they planned to spend the next day shopping and enjoying the beach.

Back at the hotel, Rachel sat on her bed with her computer to look over the video that Rusty had given her. She slowed the footage down and counted as each person passed the camera and stepped onto Randall's boat. Randall stood on the dock, patting people on the back or helping the young women on. From his actions, even though it was past midnight and he'd been in the bar all night, Randall looked quite sober.

The final man that Rusty identified as homeless came staggering down the dock. He hesitated, even though Randall waved for him to come onto the boat. As the man walked past Randall and stepped onto the ship's deck, Randall smiled wide and patted him on the back like an old friend. Was Randall just being kind, or did he have something nefarious in mind?

"What are you looking at?" Jules asked, coming out of the

bathroom, fresh from the shower. Her hair was tied up in a towel, and she was wearing pajamas.

"The video Rusty gave me. I counted twenty-four guests on the boat, counting Adrian. Twenty-five if you count the homeless man."

"Why are you counting them?" Jules asked.

"Because I want to see how many came off the boat after the party ended," Rachel said.

Jules's brows rose. "Why?"

Rachel took a deep breath and released it. "Rusty has a theory about the homeless man. I want to make sure he exited the boat before Randall took off the next day. If he, or someone else, never left the boat, then we have more than a faked death on our hands."

"Murder?" Jules asked, looking surprised.

"Possibly."

Jules sat beside Rachel, and they watched the video in fast-forward together, tallying the number of people leaving the boat. By four in the morning, everyone, even Adrian, had left the yacht—except for Randall and one man.

"Do you think Randall let the homeless man sleep it off on the boat instead of outside somewhere?" Jules asked.

"We'll find out." Rachel fast-forwarded the video through the rest of that night and into the next morning. No one left the boat. Finally, at noon, Randall stepped off the yacht and walked over to Adrian's boat. A few minutes later, Adrian followed Randall back to his yacht and was there for about an hour until he returned to his own boat. Minutes later, Randall pulled out of his slip and headed for the Gulf.

Rachel turned to Jules. "What do you think happened to the homeless man?"

Jules stared back at her with wide eyes. Rachel knew she was thinking the same thing. The homeless man became a body part floating to shore.

* * *

"Should we call the police?" Jules asked, looking pale.

"I don't know. We don't have any proof other than we didn't see him leaving on the video. Plus, the DNA that Ariel gave to the police matched the DNA of the leg that floated up to shore," Rachel said.

"What kind of sample did Ariel supply?"

"Hair from Randall's old hairbrush," Rachel said.

"It would be pretty easy to put someone else's hair in a brush, especially if he were dead," Jules said, grimacing.

Rachel sighed. "True. But it's all speculation. I can't go to Jack and give him a crazy story. He already had to put up with Ariel's drama last night."

"Have you talked to Ariel since then?" Jules asked.

Rachel shook her head. "I tried calling early this morning, but she didn't answer. I don't know if she's mad at me for having Jack come. But you'd think if she were really frightened for her life, she'd want the police involved."

"Right. Unless she is part of the whole mess."

"And there we are again—circling back to Ariel." Rachel closed her laptop and yawned. "Let's sleep on it and give it some thought. Maybe things will look clearer in the morning."

Rachel did sleep, but by morning she was just as confused as ever. She and Jules went for a nice morning walk on the beach before eating breakfast, then headed to Pier Park for a little shopping. It was nice to take some time away from Ariel's case and just enjoy the day with her daughter.

At dinnertime, Rachel suggested they eat at The Mermaid's Cove. "We can enjoy a good meal and do a little spying on Adrian at the same time," she told Jules.

"Uh, didn't that get you in trouble the last time?" Jules asked, a smirk on her face.

Rachel laughed. "This time, I'll stay off his boat."

They drove the short distance to the restaurant and requested a table outside on the second-tier balcony. The sun had nearly set, leaving streaks of orange and pink in the sky as they ordered their drinks and dinner.

"Which is his boat?" Jules asked.

Rachel pointed it out. "That one. Next to the empty slip. And two slips down and across the dock is Rusty's boat."

Jules giggled. "Rusty. Now that's a ship captain's name if I ever heard one."

Rachel chuckled along. "And he's as much a character as his name implies. But he's been a big help. Without his surveillance footage, I would never have learned about the party the night before Randall died."

As the sky darkened, the twinkle lights strung along the balcony's rail, and the lights on the yachts in the marina brightened up the inky night sky. It was charming the way nearly all the yachts had lights strung around them. As she and Jules ate their seafood dinners, Rachel didn't see any movement on Adrian's boat. There weren't any lights on. Rachel wondered if he was working tonight.

"Good evening, ladies," a male voice said, startling Rachel out of her thoughts. She spun and looked up, and there stood Jack Meyers.

Rachel studied him a moment. He was dressed casually in

cotton slacks and a short-sleeved shirt, but she had a feeling it wasn't a coincidence he was here. "Are you still following me?" she asked.

Jack laughed and shook his head. "I don't blame you for thinking that, but no, I'm not following you. But I think I had the same idea as you did." He nodded over at Adrian's boat. "Are you watching to see what he's up to?"

"You caught me," Rachel said, smiling. She introduced Jules to Jack and invited him to sit with them.

"I don't want to interrupt your dinner," Jack said.

"You aren't. We're done eating," Rachel said.

Jack joined them and ordered a beer when the waitress came to the table. "So, Jules. Are you joining your mother in amateur sleuthing?"

"Actually, I'm here for the beach and the shopping. But it's fun listening to all the details and trying to solve the mystery," Jules said.

"At this point, we're just going in circles, though," Rachel added.

"Has there been any movement around his boat?" Jack asked.

Rachel shook her head. "No. Not even a light on. That makes me believe he's not hiding Randall in there."

"Wait. What?" Jack asked, looking surprised. "You think he was hiding Randall?"

"It seemed possible," she said. Rachel explained about the footage of a man with longish hair returning to Adrian's boat the night before. "It was after the little episode at Ariel's place. What if Adrian is in on it and is dressing up as Randall to scare Ariel?"

Jack frowned. "Why would he do that?"

"To get money from her," Jules said.

Jack took a sip of his beer and pondered that a moment. "It wouldn't be too far-fetched, I suppose."

"It's all speculation right now," Rachel said. "We've been throwing around a bunch of ideas to figure out this mess."

"No matter how you look at it, though," Jack said. "It seems like Ariel is more involved than she wants anyone to believe."

Rachel and Jules exchanged a look between them.

"I saw that," Jack said, grinning. "What does it mean?"

Rachel took a deep breath. "We came up with the same conclusion last night. But it doesn't make sense. If Ariel is in on it, why hire me to dig around?"

"To throw everyone off the trail?" Jack suggested.

"But what is that?" Rachel asked. "If Randall faked his death, they have the money and can disappear. Why hire someone to look around?"

Jack sighed. "That's a good question. I guess until something else happens, there isn't much else we can do."

"We?" Rachel said, laughing. "I thought the case was closed. It's no longer yours to investigate."

"Oh, yeah? When I'm called in the middle of the night to save a woman from her dead ex-husband, I think it's become my case to investigate again. At least unofficially."

The three laughed. It was all so ridiculous they couldn't help it.

There wasn't any movement on Adrian's boat, so Jack walked Rachel and Jules to their car. "Promise me you'll be careful if you do any more investigating," Jack said quietly to Rachel. "Something fishy is going on. I don't want you to become an unsuspecting pawn in their crazy scheme."

"I'll be careful," she promised.

On the way back to the hotel, Jules eyed her mother.

"What?" Rachel asked, noticing Jules staring at her.

"That's what I'd like to know. What's going on between you and Jack Meyers?"

Rachel's eyes grew wide. "What do you mean by that? Nothing's going on. He's just helping me figure out this mess."

"Okay, Mom. But for someone who likes to solve crimes, you don't see everything clearly."

"What's that supposed to mean?" Rachel asked.

"He has a thing for you. How do you not see it?"

"Don't be crazy. Besides, Avery and I are a couple."

"Yeah. A couple who never see each other," Jules pointed out.

"Well, he's coming for Thanksgiving weekend, so then we'll be together," Rachel said.

"That's good. In the meantime, you'd better let Jack know you're taken." Jules giggled.

Rachel rolled her eyes. "You're being silly."

"Right," Jules said.

The next day, Rachel and Jules had a leisurely breakfast on their hotel room's patio and then took a final walk on the beach. Jules had to head home to get ready for school the next day, and Rachel was going to be right behind her. But first, Rachel wanted to visit Adrian one more time as well as Ariel.

After saying goodbye to Jules, Rachel headed to the marina and walked down the dock to Adrian's boat. She passed Rusty's boat and glanced up toward the camera to wave at him. That's when she noticed the camera was gone. Surprised, Rachel decided to stop by Rusty's boat after she visited with Adrian.

Standing on the dock, Rachel called out, "Adrian. Are you home?"

A minute later, Adrian came up from his quarters. "Oh. Hi." He didn't sound very enthusiastic. "What do you want?"

Rachel suddenly felt self-conscious. "I came to apologize again about going onto your boat when you weren't home. I really wasn't snooping. I thought something might have happened to you."

He nodded and waved for her to come aboard. "It's okay. After I thought about it for a while, I was flattered that you worried about me. No one worries about me. I'm not important to anyone."

"Oh." Rachel was stumped for a moment as to how to respond. "That can't be true. A young guy like you must have a few girls chasing him."

He grinned. "No. Not really. I see girls I know at the bar up at The Mermaid's Cove a lot, but there's no one special."

Rachel used his words as an opening. "I hear Randall used to have parties on his boat all the time. There were a lot of pretty girls coming down from the bar. Don't tell me he didn't invite you."

"Oh, yeah. He always invited me," Adrian said. "But I haven't met a girl who's interested in more than just a little fun. I'd like to find someone who wants a serious relationship—like Randall and Ariel's marriage. I'd much prefer that to a bunch of one-night stands."

Rachel noted the dreaminess of his tone and the faraway look in his eyes. She didn't want to burst his bubble by reminding him that Ariel and Randall had ended up divorced. "I had dinner at The Mermaid's Cove last night with my daughter. The waitress there said there was quite a party on Randall's boat the night before he died."

Adrian blinked away his dreamy stare and looked at her.

"Yeah. The bar was closing, so he invited everyone on the boat. It was so packed on there we could barely move."

"That must have been fun," Rachel said, smiling. "I was surprised it was never mentioned in the police report, though. A bunch of strangers on Randall's boat the night before he died could have been important."

Adrian's expression turned guarded. "What do you mean by that?"

"Did you ever consider that someone at the party that night might have sabotaged Randall's engine?"

Adrian sat on one of the padded benches, looking thoughtful. "No. I never thought about that, but come to think of it, I do remember something suspicious."

Rachel's heart began beating faster. Maybe someone did sabotage the engine, and Randall really was dead. "What do you remember?"

He turned and looked her straight in the eyes. "I think I know who sabotaged the yacht."

CHAPTER EIGHT

Rachel was stunned by Adrian's declaration. If he remembered something important, maybe that would solve this entire mystery. "Who?"

"I don't know his name. I'd never seen him before. I think he may have been a drifter," Adrian said. "That night, Randall had mentioned to me again about the engine trouble. The other guy heard us and said he used to be a mechanic and would be happy to look at it."

"Did he tinker with the engine that night?" Rachel asked, knowing full well that the homeless man never left the yacht after the party.

"No, not that night. The engine is in the cockpit, right under the dining table. Randall let the guy stay overnight to sleep off the alcohol, and then the man looked at the engine. He said he found something and tightened it, so Randall sent him off with a hundred-dollar bill."

Rachel frowned. "The last time I talked with you, you said you felt guilty for not fixing the engine. But now you're saying the other guy did fix it. Why did you feel guilty?"

Adrian stared at her, looking dazed, then seemed to

remember what he'd said. "Oh, that. Yeah. I should have checked the guy's work. I mean, what he did may have caused the fire. But I was too hungover to bother, and that's why I felt bad."

Hm. He seems to have an answer for everything, Rachel thought. "Do you know where the man is now?"

Adrian shrugged. "He was a drifter. I haven't seen him around since then."

Rachel nodded. "Well, thanks for talking with me again. I'm going home, so I probably won't see you for a while."

"Oh. It was nice meeting you," Adrian said. He helped her off the boat and then ducked back down below deck.

Rachel stopped by Rusty's boat and stepped aboard, calling for him. When he didn't answer, she knocked on the door of his quarters. Still, there was no answer. She wondered what had happened to his camera. Maybe someone had stolen it, and he'd gone out to buy a new one. She left a quick note thanking him for his help and slid it under the door. Then she walked back to her car up by the restaurant.

Before leaving town, Rachel stopped at Ariel's house to check on her. Ariel opened the door with a big smile and a friendly hug. It was as if the other night had never happened.

"I wanted to check on you and make sure you're okay," Rachel told her after Ariel had led her to the kitchen and poured her a glass of iced tea. Ariel was wearing a colorful billowy caftan over a swimsuit and a big floppy hat. Yet her blond hair was still dry, and her make-up was impeccable.

"Oh, I'm fine," Ariel told her, sipping her own drink. "I've been enjoying the nice weather outside by the pool with my sister."

Looking out the patio window, Rachel saw Alivia lying on

a lounge chair, and she waved to her. Alivia waved back. Unlike Ariel, her sister's hair was wet as if she'd actually swam in the pool.

"It must be nice to have a sister to spend time with," Rachel said. "I love spending time with my daughter. But I wish I'd had a sister growing up."

Ariel shrugged. "It's okay. Twins tend to get lumped together as if they're one person, so I'm used to her being around all the time."

Rachel supposed that was true. "Have you seen Randall again?"

"No, thank goodness," Ariel said. "Maybe Lieutenant Meyers scared him away. I'm sorry I was so upset that night, dear. I was surprised to see you'd called him. But now, I'm actually glad you did. Maybe Randall will stay away if he thinks I have the police on the case."

Rachel studied her, trying to figure out if she was telling the truth. It was difficult to know with Ariel because she was so dramatic. "I'm glad you're not angry with me. I only meant to help. But it didn't change anything. The case is closed as far as Jack is concerned, so he's not investigating it."

"Oh." Ariel seemed to relax after hearing this. "Well, that's good to know."

"I know the man on the tape looks like Randall, but do you think it could be someone else impersonating him to try to extort money from you?"

Ariel frowned. "I suppose someone could be. But who?"

"Well, just to throw it out there, do you think Adrian is capable of doing it?"

"Adrian?" Ariel laughed. "He's been Randall's good friend for years. And he's my friend as well. Shoot, he even used to date my sister. Why on earth would you think he'd be terrorizing me?"

Rachel shrugged, trying to appear casual about it. She was actually shocked to hear that Alivia and Adrian had once dated. Rachel had thought that Adrian had a crush on Ariel. "I was only suggesting it. Sometimes it's the people you least suspect who do these types of crimes."

Ariel's expression sobered, and she looked thoughtful. "I guess I hadn't thought of it that way. I mean, I always thought of Adrian as a teddy bear—one of those guys that didn't really have a thought in his head. But you're right. He knew Randall well."

"It was just a thought. I don't want to accuse Adrian of anything since I have no proof," Rachel said.

Ariel shook her head. "No, dear. I think it's good you brought it up. It gives me something to think about. Truthfully, if he wore a wig and dressed in dark clothing, he would look a lot like Randall."

That was what Rachel had thought, too. "There's something else I learned that I thought I'd better tell you. I talked to Randall's boss at Unified Investment Corporation, and he told me that four months before his death, Randall had been fired."

"What?" Ariel looked shocked. "Randall never told that. Why would they fire him?"

"For embezzlement. Mr. Tisdale told me Randall had stolen nearly a half-million dollars from his clients over the past few years."

Ariel paled. She looked like she was going to be physically ill. "I can't believe it," she whispered. "I didn't know." Her eyes darted up to Rachel. "But he was never prosecuted for it."

"Tisdale said they didn't want their clients to know what

had happened, so they didn't prosecute Randall. They just fired him. He didn't give me any proof that Randall stole the money—I'm only going off of what he told me."

"I…I don't know what to say," Ariel said, running a hand across her forehead. "Why would he do such a thing? He earned a good living, and I was earning well, too. I can't even fathom why he'd steal money."

"I'm sorry that I was the one to tell you this," Rachel said gently. "But you did hire me to dig up information. Apparently, the police never went to Randall's place of employment to ask questions."

"I'm glad they didn't," Ariel said. "If it had gotten out to the press that Randall had stolen money, it might have ruined my career. And I had nothing to do with it," she said, her hand covering her heart. "None of this makes sense."

"I agree," Rachel said. "But the real question is, if Randall did steal all that money, why would he be stalking you to try to get your money?"

Ariel stared at Rachel, her blue eyes wide. And then she fainted.

* * *

"Ariel! Ariel! Wake up!" Rachel had hurried to her side where she lay on the sofa, unconscious. When she didn't respond, Rachel ran to the patio door and called for Alivia, who came rushing in.

"What happened?" Alivia asked, seeing her twin lying on the sofa.

"We were talking, and she fainted. Should we call 911?" Rachel was in a near panic over Ariel's loss of consciousness.

"No. She'd hate that. Ariel's always worried about bad publicity." Alivia went to the kitchen and wet a cloth with cold water, then brought it out and began patting her sister on the face. "Wake up, Ariel," she said soothingly.

Ariel's eyelids fluttered, and she glanced around. "What happened?" she asked in a weak voice.

Rachel watched Ariel as she slowly came back to consciousness. She was beginning to wonder if her fainting had been an act. Maybe she hadn't liked Rachel's last question.

"Why don't you try to sit up?" Alivia said, helping Ariel up and propping pillows behind her.

"Oh, my. I never faint like that," Ariel said. "I'm so sorry, Rachel. What must you think of me?"

"I'm sorry if I upset you," Rachel said, watching her reaction.

"Oh, no, dear. It wasn't you. Maybe I had too much sun earlier," Ariel said.

Alivia's pale brows rose. She sniffed her sister's iced tea. "Or maybe you've had enough vodka," she said.

Rachel watched as Ariel's eyes flashed with anger. "Who can blame me for having a little to drink after all I've been through these past few weeks," she snapped at her sister. "What if Randall was stalking you?"

Alivia laughed. "You seem fine now."

"Ah! Leave me alone." Ariel pushed her sister away, and Alivia grinned as she headed back to the pool.

Rachel watched Alivia walk away. All she wore was a tiny bikini, and she certainly had the body for it. She was lean, tan, and walked gracefully like a dancer.

"Sisters!" Ariel said, sitting up straighter. "She can really drive me crazy." Her face softened as she looked over at Rachel.

"I'm sorry, dear. I do feel a bit under the weather. I think I'm going to lie down for a while."

Rachel stood, knowing that was her cue to leave. "I'll let myself out. I hope you feel better later. And I do hope your stalker—whoever he is—leaves you alone now."

"Thank you, dear," Ariel said. "And thank you for all the information you've dug up. I'll stay in touch. If you learn anything more, please call me."

"I will. Goodbye." Rachel walked out and closed the door quietly. If the camera hadn't been there, she might have been tempted to sneak a peek through the window to see if Ariel went back outside or if she did lie down. With so many windows around the house, it would have been easy to see. Instead, Rachel headed to her car. She'd watched enough drama for one day.

One thing was perfectly clear, though. The moment Rachel had asked why Randall would be stalking her if he had his own money, Ariel had put on a show to avoid answering the question. Ariel was hiding something. The big question was, what?

* * *

Rachel drove home with her stereo playing loudly so she could clear her head of Ariel's troubles for the rest of the day. She had a lot to do when she got home to prepare for Thanksgiving Day and for Avery's visit. She smiled when she thought of Avery staying for a few days. She was excited to see him and a little tentative, too. What if their relationship had cooled over the past few weeks? Would they still have that same spark they'd felt in California? She hoped so because she really liked Avery and would like to see their relationship grow.

Rachel arrived home in the late afternoon, just as the sun was going down in the west. All was quiet in her private yard as she pulled into the garage. She grabbed her suitcase and purse and headed inside. As she walked toward her bedroom, Rachel thought she heard water running.

"That's weird," she said aloud. She quickly checked the master bathroom and the hallway bathroom, but no water was on. Could she have left the hose on outside? She didn't even remember using it before she left.

Rachel walked to her studio office and through the door that led to the backyard. Instantly, she saw the hose was pulled out onto the lawn, and water was pooled around it.

Shaking her head, Rachel went to the faucet and turned it off. "I must be losing my mind," she said aloud.

She stood to walk back to the studio when a voice made her jump.

"Stop there, and don't turn around," a deep male voice demanded.

Rachel froze as her heart beat rapidly in terror.

CHAPTER NINE

Fear spread through Rachel as she stood stock still as the intruder had instructed. Who could this be? Could she run for the house and make it before the guy caught her?

"I'm not here to hurt you," the man said calmly. "So, don't get any crazy ideas. I just want to explain something to you. That's all."

"Who are you?" Rachel asked. "What do you want?"

He chuckled. "You're an inquisitive little thing, aren't you? I'm surprised you haven't guessed by now. I'm Randall Weathers."

"Randall Weathers?" Rachel was stunned. How did he know where she lived? "Why are you here?"

"I'm here because you've been snooping all over Panama City Beach asking everyone about me," he said. "And you've gotten everything wrong. I came to straighten you out."

"About what? Obviously, you faked your death," Rachel said. Her anger at him for invading her private space overrode her fear. How dare he follow her home and scare her.

Randall sighed. "I had to fake my death. Because if I hadn't, I would have been murdered."

Rachel frowned, confused. As she stared into her office window, she realized she could see his reflection behind her. His hair was slightly long and wavy, and he was wearing dark clothing. That's all she could make out. Was this Adrian pretending to be Randall? She shifted her weight onto her right leg.

"Don't even think about turning around," Randall barked. "I mean it!"

"Okay. Fine," Rachel said. She wasn't sure who it was, but she didn't want to find out what he was capable of. "Why did you have to fake your death?"

She watched as Randall started to run his hand through his hair, then thought twice about it and stopped. Was the guy wearing a wig and was afraid it would fall off?

"Because my dear ex-wife paid a man to kill me," he said.

"What?"

"It's true. The night of the party on my boat, a strange man was the last to leave. We all thought he was a homeless guy. I'd seen him wandering around the dock for a couple of months. But come to find out, he'd been paid by Ariel to kill me, then take me out into the open water and burn up the boat."

Rachel thought about this a moment. Adrian had also said the homeless man was on the boat and had spent the night. But he swore he hadn't known the man. And Rusty had also seen him several times. Had the man actually been watching Randall with the intent to kill him?

"I don't understand why Ariel would want you dead," Rachel said. "You were her ex-husband."

"Yeah. Right," Randall sounded disgusted. "But her name was still on the life insurance policy. And that woman loves money, believe me. She's the reason I kept stealing money from my clients—to keep her happy."

"Ariel claimed she knew nothing about you embezzling the money."

Randall snorted. "She not only knew but also helped me spend it. Most of it went into paying off the yacht. The rest she spent on jewelry and vacations. She was never satisfied. She insisted we have a house in the Bahamas, too, but we couldn't afford it after I was fired. So, with me dead, she could have everything she ever wanted."

Rachel shook her head. "None of this makes sense. Doesn't Ariel earn a good living from her books? She claims she does."

"Not as much money as she tries to make people think she does," Randall said. "She can probably cover the house bills and her sister's wage, and that's about it. Ariel likes living the high life. I couldn't keep up with it. The happiest day of my life was the day our divorce was finalized."

"But you made one mistake," Rachel said.

"Yep. I forgot about the life insurance policies. She didn't. She promised to pay the guy one-hundred thousand dollars to kill me and destroy the boat."

"Why didn't he kill you, then?" Rachel asked.

"Because when he pulled a gun on me that day, I did some fast talking. I'm good at that," Randall said proudly. "I talked him out of killing me and into a new plan. I promised to pay him twice as much as Ariel was to fake my death, burn the boat, and then let me scare the hell out of her."

"And is that what you're doing? Only scaring her? Or do you want something from her?" Rachel asked. In the glass, she could see Randall start to pace.

"I've already had my fun scaring her. All I want from her is half the insurance money, and I'll go away. I don't really want to hurt her." He stopped and stared at Rachel's back. "Despite everything, I still love her."

"Well, you've got a strange way of showing it," Rachel said. It was almost dark out, and she couldn't see his reflection in the window as clearly. The longer she talked with Randall, the more worried for her safety she became. Rachel just wanted to get inside her house and lock the doors and windows.

"Funny, aren't you?" he asked sarcastically. "Listen. I want you to stop investigating my death, stop talking to everyone, and definitely stay away from that cop. I want you to tell Ariel that I want one million dollars, and I'll leave her alone. Then you and she can go back to your cozy lives, and neither of you will ever see me again."

"Fine. I'll tell her," Rachel said. Anything to get him to leave.

"Tell her I'll leave a note in her mailbox explaining when and where to leave the cash," he said. "And no cops!"

Rachel nodded. "Okay." From behind, she heard heavy footsteps retreating. Rachel didn't even try to turn around and catch a glimpse of Randall. She raced into her house and locked the door.

Grabbing her phone from her purse, Rachel called Jack. "I just talked to a dead guy," she told him.

* * *

"You what?" Jack asked, clearly taken aback by what Rachel had said.

"Randall Weathers followed me home. He scared me to death," Rachel said. She walked into her bedroom and fell back on the bed. She hadn't realized how frightened she'd been until she'd locked herself inside the house. She'd begun shaking uncontrollably.

"Cripes, Rachel!" Jack said. "Are you okay?"

"Yes, I'm fine. A bit shaken up, but he kept his distance and only wanted to talk."

"Are you kidding me?" Jack sounded incensed. "He just stopped by for a chat? What the hell did he want to talk about?"

Rachel suddenly realized it had been a mistake to call Jack. What if Ariel wouldn't want the police to know what Randall wanted? But in her frightened state, Rachel's first instinct had been to call him. Now, she wasn't sure how much she should divulge.

"He just wanted to scare me off his trail," Rachel said, carefully choosing her words. "He insisted I stop investigating him and said he meant no harm to Ariel."

"Oh, well, that was nice of him," Jack said sarcastically. Then his tone softened. "Do you want me to come over there so you're not alone?"

"Oh, no. I couldn't ask you to drive two hours just because some lunatic scared me," she said. "I'm fine."

"Are you sure?" Jack asked. "I hate to think of you being home alone after such a scare. It wouldn't be a problem at all."

Suddenly, her daughter's words earlier in the week rushed back to Rachel. *He has a thing for you,* Jules had said after meeting Jack. Rachel had thought her daughter was being silly at the time, but now, she wondered. Jack was offering to drive two hours across Florida at night to protect her. Maybe it was more personal for him than for her.

"Thank you, Jack, but I'll be fine," Rachel said. "He's gone now, and I'm locked inside my house. He can't bother me now."

There was a long pause on the other end of the line before

Jack spoke up again. "Do you know if it was Randall for certain? Did you get a good look at him?"

Rachel described what had happened and how she'd only seen his reflection in the window. "There was one odd thing, though," she said. "It was like he was wearing a wig. He was going to run his hand through his hair but stopped himself. And I've seen Adrian make the same gesture, even though his hair is quite short. I don't know. It made me wonder."

"You think Adrian might be behind all of this and is wearing a disguise?" Jack asked.

Rachel sighed. "I'm not sure. It didn't sound like Adrian, but he could have disguised his voice. I have no proof one way or the other."

"Okay. I'll drop by Adrian's boat tomorrow and see what I can learn," Jack said. "I'll also ask for the camera footage from The Mermaid's Cove to see if there's anything on Adrian's comings and goings."

"You might want to check with Rusty Garrett, too. He has a camera on his boat and may have some interesting footage. Just tell him you know me."

Jack chuckled. "So, he's a close personal friend of yours?"

"Ha, ha. I think he'd be more willing to help you if he thinks he's helping me, too," Rachel said.

"Okay. I'll stop there too." Jack paused a moment. "I know you wanted to keep this secret, but I'd like to file an official report on this just to back up my reasons for investigating it. Do you mind?"

Rachel thought about this. She felt that Randall invading her private property was crossing a line. This was no longer just Ariel's problem; it was hers. "Yes. Go ahead. Do I need to report it to local police?"

"No. I can take it from here," Jack said, sounding relieved. "I'm going to press Ariel to submit a report too. I need a good reason to reopen this investigation. Do you think she'll go along with that?"

"I don't know," Rachel said. "She wanted all this to be a secret. You could try, though."

Rachel described what happened again and gave Jack the timeline to the best of her knowledge. Once she'd hung up, she sat on the bed, not sure what to do. She hadn't told Jack everything, and she felt guilty about it. What if Randall did mean to harm Ariel? If what he'd said was true, Ariel had hired a paid killer to do away with Randall. Her ex-husband could decide to turn around and do the same thing to her.

Lifting her phone, Rachel texted Ariel. "We have to meet tomorrow."

* * *

Rachel and Ariel chose to meet at a little mom-and-pop café on Main Street in the little town of Blountstown. It was roughly halfway between their places. Rachel didn't want to communicate by phone and definitely not speak at Ariel's house in case someone was listening. Rachel knew it sounded paranoid to think that her or Ariel's house was bugged. But after last night, she didn't want to take any chances. A neutral place was best.

Rachel arrived at two o'clock—the appointed time—and picked a booth at the back of the café, ordering a glass of iced tea. A few minutes later, Ariel arrived wearing a dark pantsuit, sunglasses, and a scarf around her head. Rachel would have laughed at her disguise if the situation hadn't been so dire.

Ariel sat across from Rachel and pulled off the sunglasses

and scarf. She ordered tea from the waitress, then leaned over the table. "So, what is all this cloak and dagger stuff about?" she asked, looking serious.

"Randall visited me at my house last night," Rachel said. "He had a message for you."

Ariel's hands flew to her mouth. "Oh, no! Is that why Lieutenant Meyers was at my door early this morning? You must have called him."

Rachel was both surprised and angered that Ariel was more worried about Jack showing up than about the message Randall had for her. "Yes. He's opening the case up again so he can officially investigate it. This has become serious, Ariel," she said gravely. "He's no longer bothering only you; he was at my house!"

Ariel had the good grace to look sheepish. "I'm sorry, Rachel. Of course, it's serious. I didn't mean to imply it wasn't. What did Randall say to you?"

"First of all, did you hire a hitman to kill Randall and destroy his yacht?"

Ariel's blue eyes widened. She reached for the gold sun charm hanging on a long chain around her neck and started fidgeting with it. "No! Of course not! How could you even ask me that?"

Rachel calmed a little, feeling guilty for asking her that question. "I'm sorry, but Randall told me that you had. And said that was why he faked his death. Now," she glanced around to make sure no one else was listening. Lowering her voice, Rachel said, "Now he wants you to give him a million dollars to disappear for good."

"A million dollars!" Ariel screeched. Her hand flew to her mouth once she realized she'd said it so loudly. "A million dollars?" she whispered. "Why would I give him that much money? He's supposed to be dead."

Rachel studied Ariel's reaction. She did seem to be surprised about Randall wanting the money. But was she acting? Rachel could no longer tell. "Apparently, he's very much alive and wants half the money you received from the life insurance. He said he offered the hitman twice what you had so as not to kill him. He won't bother you anymore if you give him the money."

The waitress brought Ariel's tea, and she started fiddling with her cup and spoon. "I…I don't know what to say," Ariel murmured. She looked Rachel straight in the eyes. "I did not hire someone to kill Randall. I swear."

Rachel was almost certain she believed her. Almost. "Okay. But what about the money? Are you going to give it to him?"

Ariel sighed and took a sip of the hot liquid. Her coral lipstick left a smudge on the rim of the cup. "I suppose I'll have to. I figured that was why he was stalking me, but I don't understand why he faked his death. Maybe it was for the money all along."

"It is a lot of money," Rachel said, sitting back against the booth. "I'm not sure if it's worth faking your death for, though. Are you sure it couldn't be someone else pretending to be Randall in order to blackmail you?"

Ariel shook her head, her blond bob swaying back and forth. "The man I saw in my yard and on my security camera was Randall. I'd know him anywhere—even in the dark. He must have become so desperate for money that he thought this was the only way to get it. It's so disheartening to think that I was married to him for ten years and had no clue who he really was."

Rachel reached across the table and placed her hand on her

friend's arm. "I'm sorry."

Ariel gave her a wan smile. "Thank you, dear. And thank you for sticking by me through all this. I'm sorry I dragged you into this mess and that he scared you last night. But now I know what he wants, and I can deal with that."

"Are you going to give him the money?" Rachel asked.

"What choice do I have?" Ariel said, looking forlorn. "If it will make him go away, it'll be worth it."

Rachel nodded but still thought it was strange. Something was off. Way off.

Ariel's eyes grew wide. "Did you tell Lieutenant Meyers what Randall wanted?"

"No, I didn't. I realized after calling him that you might not want him to know. Especially the part about you supposedly hiring a hitman to kill your ex."

Ariel sighed with relief. "Thank you. This morning when he stopped by, he didn't say anything about Randall wanting money. I just want to pay Randall off and put this whole thing behind me."

"But what if it isn't Randall?" Rachel persisted. "If you pay the person, he could come after you for more money. It might never end."

Ariel shook her head slowly. "No. It's Randall. I'm sure of it. And if he says he's not here to hurt me and only wants the money, I believe him. He may be a jerk, but he's always kept his word to me."

Rachel told her the instructions Randall had given her, and then they parted after hugging in the parking lot.

"Don't worry about me," Ariel said, smiling at Rachel. "I'll be fine. You enjoy your Thanksgiving holiday and don't give me a second thought. I'm a survivor."

Rachel nodded, thinking that was really the opposite of what Ariel was. Ariel was ethereal, a bit flighty, and a wonderful storyteller. But she didn't seem strong enough to Rachel to be a survivor.

Rachel drove home, stopping at the grocery store to pick up a few last-minute items for Thanksgiving dinner. The entire time, she couldn't stop thinking about Ariel's situation. Something was bothering her, but she just couldn't put her finger on it. An eerie feeling fell over her on the way home that she couldn't shake off.

CHAPTER TEN

The house felt festive as Rachel prepared for the Thanksgiving weekend. She'd put up the Christmas tree and trimmings because she loved the holidays and wanted to enjoy the decorations. She baked sugar cookies and pumpkin bread and planned on making both an apple and a pumpkin pie for Thursday's dinner. But most of all, she was excited to finally see Avery after all these weeks.

Rachel had decided to push aside Ariel's situation for the weekend so she could enjoy her holiday. She'd also decided she'd connect with Ariel one last time to return her check. Now that Jack was investigating the case again, Rachel felt that she shouldn't keep the money. She didn't want any part of it.

Wednesday afternoon, Rachel and Jules visited Aunt Julie at the memory care center and ate lunch with her since they wouldn't see her on Thanksgiving Day. Julie looked older every time Rachel saw her, and it broke her heart. Julie's memory was fading just as quickly. As they were leaving, Julie looked at them almost as if she recognized them, but then her eyes faded again. Rachel was thankful she and Jules could spend time with Julie because she wasn't sure how much time her aunt would be with them.

On Wednesday night, Rachel dressed carefully, putting on a light touch of make-up and curling the ends of her hair. She drove the forty minutes to Tallahassee International Airport and waited anxiously for Avery's plane to arrive. Rachel didn't have to wait long—it taxied in right on time, and soon he was striding toward her with a big grin on his face.

Avery stopped when he reached her, and they smiled at each other. "I'm here," he said.

"You're here," she said, smiling.

Avery reached out and pulled her into his arms, holding her tightly. Rachel knew in that moment there would be no awkwardness between them. Being in his arms felt like going home.

Avery had only brought a carry-on bag, so they headed to her car, and she drove back to the house. As they talked non-stop, catching up on all the little details of each other's lives, Rachel stole glances of Avery. She'd nearly forgotten how handsome he was and how fit he kept himself for his job as an FBI agent. His wavy brown hair was freshly cut, and the gold flecks in his warm brown eyes sparkled as he looked at her.

"I'm so glad you're here," Rachel said as she pulled into her driveway.

He reached over and ran his hand through her hair, making shivers run down her spine. "Me, too," he said huskily.

They went inside, and she showed him to the master bedroom where he could put his bag. "Unless you'd rather be in a guest room," she teased.

"Not on your life." Avery pulled her close then and kissed her deeply. "I don't want to miss a moment of being next to you."

She laughed. "Sounds a little stalkerish if you ask me," she said.

Avery opened a bottle of red wine, and the couple sat in the living room in front of the Christmas tree, eating cheese and crackers and drinking the wine. It was so nice being together again that they couldn't keep their hands off one another.

"I hope I'm not keeping you from baking something delicious for tomorrow," he said, kissing her neck suggestively. "I'd hate to miss out on pie."

She laughed. "Don't worry, you'll get your dessert."

"I don't think I can wait," he said, kissing her again. He rose and offered her his hand. "I think I have jetlag and need to go to bed."

"Jetlag from a two-hour flight?" Rachel said. But she smiled and took his hand.

He pretended to yawn, which made her laugh, and they walked to the bedroom hand in hand.

* * *

The next morning Rachel had the turkey and side dishes cooking by the time Jules showed up. Avery was outside, tacking up strings of Christmas lights on the house.

"Did you meet Avery?" Rachel asked her daughter when she walked into the kitchen.

Jules laughed. "Yes, I did. I can't believe you talked him into putting up the lights."

"I didn't make him do it," Rachel protested. "He offered. But it will be nice to have lights up for a change. So, what did you think of him?"

"I think that any man who's willing to put up lights for you is a keeper," Jules said, grinning. "Poor Lieutenant Meyers will be heartbroken."

Avery came inside at that exact moment. "Why will Lieutenant Meyers be heartbroken?"

"Just ignore her," Rachel said. "She's teasing me." Rachel pulled a platter of cut-up veggies and dip from the refrigerator and placed it on the counter with a bag of chips. "Here. Eat up. This is all the lunch I'm making."

The three of them snacked on the food as Avery and Jules got to know each other. Rachel basted the turkey and bustled around, happy to have the two people she cared most about together in the same room.

"Has Mom caught you up on the Ariel Weathers's case?" Jules asked Avery. "I haven't heard the latest."

"We don't want to talk about that today," Rachel said.

Avery studied her a moment. "I'd like to hear about it. Have you learned anything new about Randall?"

Both Jules and Avery watched her in anticipation. Rachel sighed. "I've decided to back out of the case. Jack has reopened it, and there's no more reason for me to be poking around."

"Really," Avery said, raising one brow. "I've only worked on one case with you, but I know you wouldn't stop unless something happened. Spill."

"Yeah, Mom. We spent a whole weekend there just to help Ariel. Why are you giving up so soon?"

Rachel hesitated. She hadn't planned on telling Jules or Avery about her surprise visit from Randall. It would only upset them. But she knew she should be completely honest with them, considering she'd already dragged them both into Ariel's drama. "Okay. But don't get upset because I'm here, and I'm fine," she began.

Avery frowned. "That already upsets me. What happened?"

First, Rachel filled them in on her visit with Adrian and

Ariel that past Sunday before she headed home from the beach. Then she finally admitted that Randall had been waiting for her in the back yard at the house.

"Mom! Are you kidding?" Jules looked fearful. "Weren't you scared?"

"It all happened so fast that I didn't have time to be scared until I came back inside after he'd left," Rachel said. "That was the last straw, though. I don't want anything else to do with it."

Avery was silent, but Rachel could tell he was upset. "You should have called me to tell me about it," he said gently. "I hate to think that you were here alone and scared, and I wasn't here to help."

Rachel placed her hand over his. "There was no reason to call you or Jules. It would have only upset you both. I was safe, and I did call Jack to report it. He's taking the lead on it now."

"Well, I guess that's good," Avery said, eyeing Rachel. "And I'm glad you're backing away. It's become too dangerous."

"Yeah, Mom. I'm glad too. We don't want a dead man bothering you," Jules said.

The three of them stared at each other, and then Jules began to giggle. Avery and Rachel joined in. "I didn't mean for it to be funny," Jules said, still laughing.

"I know, dear. But it is. The whole case is ridiculous," Rachel said. "Now, let's forget all about it and enjoy the day." She looked over at Avery. "Did you hang all the lights?"

"Okay. Okay. I'm going," he said. He kissed her lightly on the head before heading outside.

Jules pulled a face. "Are you two going to be all mushy and stupid?"

Rachel grinned at her daughter. "I hope so."

They had a delicious meal that evening, and Rachel was

relieved that her daughter liked Avery. By the time Jules was getting ready to head home, Rachel could tell she had her approval.

"He's really nice, Mom," Jules said as she hugged her goodbye.

"Does it bother you that I'm seeing him?" Rachel asked as she pulled away. It had been years since Jules's father had passed away, but she didn't want her to be uncomfortable about her mother dating.

Jules smiled. "No. Not at all. I don't expect you to be alone forever."

Rachel hugged her again. "Thanks, sweetheart. Your opinion means a lot to me."

"Did I pass the daughter test?" Avery asked when Rachel returned to the kitchen. He was placing their dessert plates in the dishwasher.

"With flying colors," she said. "And if you keep doing the dishes, I won't ever let you leave."

He laughed, and they went out to the living room to snuggle on the sofa.

"I am worried about that guy who showed up in your yard. Whether he's Randall or an impersonator, it's scary to think you're on his radar now," Avery said, draping his arm around her shoulders.

Rachel snuggled in closer. "I don't think you have to worry. It had more to do with Ariel than with me. And I think she's decided to pay the guy off, so hopefully, he'll be gone."

"Hopefully," Avery said. "Do you really believe it's as cut and dried as all that?"

She shook her head. "Not really. It seems like a big, twisted mess, and I can't for the life of me figure out why I was pulled into it."

Avery stood and grinned. "For now, I'm going to pull you into something that will take your mind off of that mess." He reached for her hand and pulled her off the sofa and into a hug. It didn't take long for Rachel to forget about Ariel once they entered her bedroom.

* * *

Rachel and Avery spent Friday and Saturday playing tourist, visiting a few of the sites around Tallahassee. They strolled hand-in-hand along St. Mark's Historic Railroad Trail, keeping out of the way of the many serious bikers. They also visited the Mission San Luis de Apalachee, where they wandered the church and other buildings and perused the many exhibits of native artwork. Saturday night, the couple ate at a quaint seafood place not far from Rachel's home, relaxing and talking. They never lacked for conversation. Rachel liked the comfortable way Avery fit into her life—it was as if they'd been together for years, not just a few weeks.

Sunday morning, the magic of the four-day holiday was fading. Rachel dreaded saying goodbye to Avery, who was leaving on the late-night flight back to Baltimore.

"I hate to see you go," she said as they lay in bed together, tangled in the sheets.

"I wish I could stay longer." Avery kissed her sweetly on the cheek. "Four days wasn't long enough."

Rachel agreed. They rose, and Avery made omelets for them, then they sat outside on the brick patio in the private backyard.

"This is really a beautiful place," Avery said, glancing around.

"Thanks. I like it. You should see the trees bloom in the spring. It's magical."

He grinned over at her. "I plan to."

They planned to stop for dinner before Rachel dropped Avery off at the airport that evening. He packed, and they spent nearly every second together. Around three o'clock in the afternoon, her phone rang.

"It's Jack," she said, looking up at Avery. "I wonder what he wants."

"A date?" he teased, eyebrows waggling.

She rolled her eyes and answered lightly. "Hi, Jack. What's up?"

"Rachel," he said in his serious detective voice. "I thought I'd better call you before you see it on the news."

Rachel's heart pounded. "What?"

"Ariel Weathers is dead."

CHAPTER ELEVEN

"What?" Rachel almost dropped the phone. She couldn't believe she'd heard Jack right. Avery came immediately to her side.

"I'm sorry, but I thought it would be best for me to tell you," Jack said. "She was found earlier today, floating in the swimming pool at her home. I'm still there now."

Rachel moved to the sofa and sat down, and Avery did also. She was having a hard time accepting that Ariel was dead. "This doesn't make sense. Randall promised he wouldn't hurt her."

"If it was Randall," Jack said.

Rachel understood. It could be someone posing as Randall. "I feel terrible," she said. "I never truly believed Randall would kill her. I even thought she might have been involved in all of it." She shook her head as tears filled her eyes. "Who found her?"

"Her sister, Alivia, I'm afraid," Jack said. "I haven't questioned her yet because she was hysterical, but she came home from staying at a friend's place overnight and found Ariel in the pool. Poor woman."

"That's awful," Rachel said, her tears tumbling down her cheeks. Avery wrapped his arm around her.

"Listen," Jack said. "I can't talk now, but I was wondering if you could come to Panama City Beach Tuesday or Wednesday so you and I could compare notes. We need to catch this guy, whoever he is."

"Yes. Anything to help." Rachel swiped at her tears with her hand.

"Good. I'll call you tomorrow when I get a chance. We're canvassing the neighborhood to see if anyone saw or heard something, and I've asked Alivia for Ariel's security camera footage. It's going to be a long night."

"Good luck," she said sadly.

"And Rachel?"

"Yes?"

"Please make sure your doors and windows are locked. I hate thinking of you there alone with some crazy person running around free," Jack said.

"I will." She looked up at Avery, thankful he was here at this moment. "Someone is with me, so I'll be fine."

"Okay. Talk to you later." Jack hung up, and Rachel ended the call.

"Did something happen to Ariel?" Avery asked.

She nodded. "She's dead. They found her floating in the pool."

"That's awful!"

She nodded and curled up into him. It was terrible. She wished now that she'd told Jack about Randall's demand for money and Ariel's insistence that she'd take care of it. Something must have happened to make Randall—or whoever it was—angry enough to kill Ariel.

"Do they have any suspects?" Avery asked.

She shook her head. "You mean other than her dead ex-husband? Jack said he hadn't gotten that far yet. He still has to talk to Ariel's twin sister, Alivia, and look for any witnesses. I'm sure his superior would fire him on the spot if Jack claimed a dead man had killed her."

"Wow. This is crazy. That poor woman," Avery said.

Rachel sat up. "Jack wants me to come there this week so we can exchange notes on what we both know. I'm afraid I kept some important information from him, for Ariel's sake. Now, I wish I'd told him. Maybe they could have stopped this from happening."

"It wasn't your fault, Rachel. She asked you to keep the money exchange quiet. It was her choice, not yours," Avery said.

Rachel nodded. "Still, I wish I had said something."

"I'm staying a few more days," Avery announced. "I can't leave you alone when there's a crazy killer out there who has already snuck up on you once."

"I can't ask you to stay," Rachel protested. "You have work."

"You didn't ask, I offered. I couldn't live with myself if I left tonight. And I'm certainly not going to let you go to Panama City Beach alone until they catch her murderer."

"Normally, I'd fight you on this, but to tell the truth, I'm relieved you want to stay. This was much more than I'd bargained for when Ariel asked a favor of me."

Avery held her close again. "I'm sorry that all this happened, sweetie. And I'm happy to stay. It won't be the first time we've been in a scary situation."

She gave him a small smile. "That's for sure."

Rachel called Jules to update her on what had happened to Ariel before it hit the nightly news. Her daughter was shocked and told her mother how sorry she was.

"What about you, Mom? Are you safe?"

"I'll be fine," Rachel said, glancing over at Avery, who'd taken it upon himself to pour them both a beer. "Avery is going to stay a little longer."

Jules was relieved to hear that. After Rachel hung up, she accepted the beer from Avery and took a sip.

"I think we need something stronger," Avery said. "But this will do."

That evening, they turned on the news and saw that Ariel's death was already the top story. Even though the details hadn't yet been released by the police, the news anchor was speculating on a number of things, all of them wrong. Rachel thought it was disrespectful of them to make up stories about a person they knew nothing about.

Rachel and Avery stayed close to home on Monday. Neither was in the mood to go anywhere. Jack called Rachel late in the afternoon.

"You're going to love this," he said after she'd answered. "You'll never guess where Alivia was Friday night through Sunday morning."

Rachel frowned. "Where?"

"On Adrian's boat."

His answer hit her like a brick. "Are you kidding me?"

"No. She gave Adrian as her alibi, which then makes her his alibi."

Rachel pondered that. Again, it all seemed too tidy. "Have you learned anything else?"

"Ariel definitely drowned. There was water in her lungs. We have to wait for the coroner's report, though, and toxicology. Alivia said Ariel had been drinking a lot lately and taking sleeping pills at night. It may have just been an accident."

"Do you believe that?" Rachel asked.

"Not on your life," Jack said with certainty. "Can you meet me for lunch tomorrow around one at The Mermaid's Cove? We have a lot to talk about."

"Sure." She glanced over at Avery. She decided not to mention he'd be joining them.

"Great. Be safe, okay?"

"I will."

After the call ended, Rachel told Avery everything Jack had said.

"Did you notice if Ariel was drinking too much?" Avery asked.

Rachel thought back to the last time she was at Ariel's house to check on her. Ariel had fainted, and she remembered Alivia sniffing Ariel's iced tea and commenting that vodka was in it. "Hm. Her sister alluded to the fact that Ariel was drinking when I was there. Ariel was angry at her for saying it. But I just can't imagine Ariel falling into the pool. She was very meticulous about her hair and makeup. And she didn't like sunning herself because it freckled her skin. She wore a big hat, sunglasses, and a flowing caftan over her swimsuit the day I saw her."

Avery looked thoughtful. "That's interesting. Be sure to write down any details you remember so you can tell the Lieutenant. It's all important in a murder case."

They were just about to sit down to dinner —food they'd had delivered—when Avery's phone buzzed. He walked into the other room to answer and then came back scowling.

"What's wrong?" Rachel asked.

"That was my boss. I have to get back to Baltimore tonight. There's an important case that's opened up, and he wants me on it pronto. I tried to stall a couple of days, but he insisted." Avery ran his hand through his hair. "I'm sorry, Rachel. I hate leaving you here alone."

She walked over and wrapped her arms around him. "It's okay. Your work is important. And I've decided to stay in Panama City Beach for a couple of days, so I'll be fine. I want to make sure I help Jack in any way possible."

Avery sighed but nodded. "Okay. But don't let two things happen."

Her brows furrowed. "What two things?"

"Don't get killed by a lunatic, and don't fall for that Lieutenant."

She laughed. "I promise I won't let either happen."

Avery insisted on getting an Uber to drive him to the airport so Rachel could stay safely at home. They stood in the foyer, holding each other close before his car came.

"I'm really going to miss you," she said. "I'm already looking forward to the next time we're together."

"I'm going to miss you, too," he said sadly. "I loved being here with you. I wish I could stay and help you with this case."

"Me, too."

They kissed goodbye, and Rachel continued to stare out the front door long after Avery's car had disappeared.

* * *

Rachel was up early the next morning and drove the two hours to Panama City Beach. She rented a room in the same hotel she'd stayed at before—a much smaller, cheaper room—then headed to The Mermaid's Cove. She wanted to arrive a few minutes early so she could talk to Rusty before lunch.

Rachel walked down the dock, enjoying the feel of the sun. It was a beautiful day—low humidity and warm sunshine—one of those perfect days that made you happy you lived in Florida. As she approached Rusty's boat, she glanced in the direction of Adrian's. There was no movement onboard. She supposed that if Alivia were in a relationship with Adrian, he'd be comforting her at the house.

"Ahoy there!" Rusty called from his boat, a broad grin on his bearded face. "I didn't think I'd see you for a while."

Rachel smiled. There was something about Rusty that made him instantly likable. Today he was wearing yet another faded Hawaiian shirt and cargo shorts with old-fashioned deck shoes on his feet. "Ahoy," she yelled back. "I thought I'd check in with you while I was in town."

"Well, come aboard." He offered her his hand, and she stepped aboard, thankful she'd had the good sense to wear flat shoes.

"Did you get my note?" she asked after they'd sat on deck chairs.

"I did. I think that was one of the days I had to go out and buy another security camera," Rusty said. "I've had three so far. Someone keeps pulling them down and breaking them, no matter how high I mount them."

"Really? Why would anyone do that?" Rachel asked.

Rusty's eyes went to Adrian's boat. "I wondered the same thing. So I got smart and put a new one up and a second one was hidden facing the first camera."

Rachel leaned forward. "Did you catch the culprit?"

Rusty nodded. "I did. It was none other than pretty boy across the way." He pointed toward Adrian's boat.

"Adrian?" Rachel wasn't as stunned as she should have

been. She knew he was hiding something but had no proof. "Why do you think he did it?"

"I have no idea, little lady. But I have video of him vandalizing my boat that I may take to the police." Rusty lowered his voice. "I'm sure you've heard about the Weathers woman being killed."

"Yes. That's the reason I'm here."

"Right. Well, Adrian's been coming and going a lot, starting with the weekend she was murdered. He had a woman there with him, too. A little blond number."

Rachel's brows flew up. "What? Don't you mean a redhead?"

Rusty stroked his long beard as he thought. "Well, I may have gotten the color wrong. It was dark out when I saw them. Anyway, she stayed a couple of nights, and each night my camera was destroyed. I have a feeling Adrian didn't want anyone to see them together."

Rachel nodded. She couldn't think of any reason Adrian and Alivia would care that their movements were caught on camera. Unless they were guilty of something. That feeling Rachel had before—that something was off—came back.

"I think you should hang on to that video of Adrian breaking your camera. I'll tell Lieutenant Meyers about it in case he thinks it's relevant," Rachel told Rusty.

"And speak of the devil," Rusty said, standing up. "I'll bet you're Lieutenant Meyers."

Rachel turned and saw Jack standing on the dock, looking up at them.

"Hello. You must be Rusty Garrett," Jack said. "You're not trying to steal my lunch date, are you?"

Rusty snorted. "An old coot like me has no chance with a pretty lady like Rachel."

Rachel said goodbye to Rusty, but not before giving him her phone number in case he saw anything strange again. Jack also gave him his card. The two walked up to the restaurant and chose an outdoor table facing the marina.

"I want to see if Adrian shows up," Jack said. "I'm in the process of getting a search warrant for his boat. We need to see if he's playing host to his dead best friend, Randall."

Rachel told him about Rusty's video of Adrian breaking his security camera.

Jack pondered this. "Well, that makes sense now. The restaurant's camera that overlooks the marina is broken too. They haven't bothered to replace it."

"All of this points the finger at Adrian being guilty," Rachel said. "I guess he could have been impersonating Randall. But I don't believe he'd kill Ariel. I think he had a crush on her."

"Interesting." Jack looked surprised. "But why was he supposedly with Alivia?"

The waitress came and took their order, then returned with their drinks. After they were alone again, they continued their conversation.

"Ariel mentioned that her sister had dated Adrian for a while. It was when I was at her house before leaving Panama City Beach the first time," Rachel said.

"Do you think they're still together? Or was she just using him as an excuse to leave her sister for the weekend?" Jack asked.

"I really don't know." Rachel fiddled with the straw in her Coke glass before making a confession. "I didn't tell you everything Randall said to me the night he showed up in my backyard. Now, I wish I had. It might have saved Ariel's life."

Jack leaned in closer. "You can tell me now," he said gently.

Rachel looked into Jack's eyes. They were brown like Avery's but a different shade of brown. Darker. But they were kind eyes, despite his tough job. Jack hadn't let working homicides make him cynical. She thought that was a sign of a strong personality.

"He said he didn't want to hurt Ariel. He wanted one million dollars, and he'd leave her alone."

Jack's brows rose. "Half of the insurance money?"

She nodded. "But there's more. Randall told me he faked his death because Ariel had hired a hitman to kill him. So, he made a deal with the hitman to pay him double what Ariel was paying him and to help him fake his death. Unbelievable, don't you think?"

Jack shook his head. "This story gets weirder and weirder. Would Ariel have really had her ex-husband killed to collect two million dollars? I thought she was earning a good income on her own."

"It was more than the life insurance," Rachel said. "There was also the insurance on the boat. That would have been somewhere between three to four hundred thousand dollars."

"Okay. I do remember her receiving money for that, too," Jack said. "Still, to be so greedy as to kill your ex for money. It's insane."

The waitress brought their lunch and left. Jack took a bite of his hamburger, looking thoughtful, like he was trying to figure everything out.

Rachel ate a small bite of her BLT sandwich, then wiped her mouth. "Did you ever talk to Randall's employer?"

"No. Randall had quit before he died. There was no reason to talk to him."

"Randall hadn't quit. He'd been fired. For embezzling

nearly five-hundred thousand dollars."

"What?" Jack set his burger down and stared at her, stunned. "How do you know that?"

She grinned. "I went to talk to his boss. He was also surprised no one from the police force came to ask him questions."

Jack cleared his throat, looking embarrassed. "Well, I guess I fumbled that one. But why wasn't it ever reported to the police that he'd stolen so much money?"

"His boss, Roger Tisdale, said the company couldn't afford for their investors to learn that money had been stolen. The company covered the lost funds and tossed Randall out. Roger thought that Randall used the money to pay off the yacht and keep up the pretense of a rich lifestyle. He sort of blamed it on Ariel."

Jack wiped his hands on his napkin and pulled a little notepad and pen from his jacket pocket. "I need to take notes. You seem to have investigated Randall's death better than I did."

Rachel laughed. "I just went to all the logical places. I told Ariel about Randall embezzling the money, and she seemed surprised about it. But you know, when I think back at the few times I spoke with her, she seemed to be acting. Like she knew more than she would tell."

"Which could have been the reason she was killed," Jack said earnestly.

"Maybe." Rachel wondered if that was what had killed her or if she'd really been stalked and killed by her ex husband. Or some other crazy person looking to get her money. "Do you know yet when Ariel's funeral is?"

Jack shook his head. "The coroner probably won't release the body for at least a week. Then Alivia will be able to bury her."

Rachel felt a chill crawl up her spine and physically shook. "I hate thinking about Ariel having an autopsy. It's creepy. I just spoke to her a week ago. And now she's gone. It's still hard to wrap my head around."

"I know," Jack said gently. "I was shocked when I first heard she'd been killed. And it wasn't easy going to the murder scene, either. But that's what I do."

Rachel winced. "Can I ask you something? Was Ariel in a swimsuit when she was found or wearing clothes?"

Jack seemed surprised by her question. "A swimsuit. There was a long dress-like thing hanging over a lounge chair as if she'd removed it to go into the pool."

"Was there a glass of iced tea or some type of drink near the pool?" Rachel asked.

Jack frowned as he thought about that. "Yes, I think there was. Just one glass, though. It was taken into evidence to check if any type of drug was in it. Why?"

"Sunday was a warm day," Rachel said. "And I know for a fact that Ariel didn't like laying in the sun because it freckled her skin. She was also very particular about her makeup and hair. I guess I was surprised she was in the pool at all."

Jack nodded. "That's what we're trying to find out. If she fell in accidentally, or someone held her under the water."

They finished their meal and turned the conversation to other topics. Talking about Ariel's death was getting too morbid.

"Are you heading home after this?" Jack asked.

"No. I'm staying at the same hotel as last time, at least overnight. I didn't know if there was anything I could do to help."

"You've already helped a lot," Jack said, smiling. "Maybe we could meet for dinner later?"

She was just about to answer when his phone rang. Jack pulled it out of his pocket and answered. When he was done, he was grinning.

"I just got permission to search Adrian's boat. Let's go."

CHAPTER TWELVE

Rachel followed Jack out of the restaurant and down to the dock. They waited for an officer to bring the paperwork.

"What do you think you'll find?" Rachel asked.

Jack shrugged. "I'm not sure. Randall hiding in a closet, maybe." He smiled. "Or a wig and dark clothes. Or maybe nothing. Adrian could be just a pawn in Randall's game. If I don't find anything, I'm back to believing a dead man killed his ex-wife."

Rachel knew how he felt. They were running around in circles.

The officer arrived, and Rachel followed him and Jack down to Adrian's boat. She stayed near Rusty's boat while Jack went aboard Adrian's and banged on the cabin door. Rusty popped up from his quarters, staring at Rachel with raised brows.

"Lieutenant Meyers has a warrant to search Adrian's boat," she explained.

"About time," Rusty mumbled.

From her spot on the dock, Rachel watched as a befuddled-looking Adrian finally unlocked the door. His clothes were rumpled, and he looked terrible.

"What's going on?" he asked groggily. "I was sleeping."

"I'm Lieutenant Jack Meyers from the Panama City Beach Police," Jack said in his official voice. "I have a warrant to search your boat." He handed Adrian the folded piece of paper.

"What?" Adrian looked at the men with glassy eyes. From her vantage point, Rachel wondered if he'd been sleeping off a bender. "Why?"

"Because we have cause to believe you may be involved in the death of Ariel Weathers," Jack told him. "Please step aside and let us search."

At this, Adrian's eyes widened. "How could you possibly think I had anything to do with Ariel's death? Ariel was my friend. I cared about her. I'd never hurt her."

"Are you going to let us search, or will we have to arrest you?" Jack asked sternly.

Looking dumbfounded, Adrian stepped aside and went to sit on one of the outdoor benches. Rachel watched as Adrian dropped his head in his hands, and suddenly, her heart went out to him. Maybe he was completely innocent and really had no idea what was going on. Or maybe he was being set up as the fall guy.

"What're you thinking there, missy?" Rusty asked.

"I'm beginning to think Adrian hasn't done anything wrong."

"He broke at least two of my cameras as far as I know. What was he trying to hide?" Rusty asked.

"I don't know. Maybe he was just tired of you watching his every move. Or maybe he was hiding something. I guess we'll see soon."

Rachel watched as Jack and the other officer finally came out from the cabin. His hands were empty, so it looked like he hadn't found anything incriminating. "Where were you yesterday and last night?" Jack asked Adrian.

Adrian lifted his head. "I was with Alivia at Ariel's house for a while yesterday, then I went to work. I worked a sunset cruise for tourists. After that, I sat in the bar near that marina for a couple of hours. I drank way too much, so I had an Uber drive me back here."

"And where were you the day Ariel Weathers died?" Jack asked.

A pained expression fell over Adrian's face. "I was here at the marina, on my boat. But you already know that because Alivia told you she was here with me."

Rachel watched as Jack clenched his jaw. She knew immediately that he was angry he hadn't found anything.

"Don't leave town. I may have more questions for you," Jack said. He waved at the other officer to follow him, and they both left the boat.

Rachel watched as Adrian glared at the detective's back, then dragged himself back inside his quarters, shutting the door behind him.

Rachel met with Jack as the other officer walked up the dock to his car.

"Well, that was a waste of time," Jack said. "His boat was clean. Nothing to connect him to any of it."

"He's smarter than he looks, I guess," Rusty broke in. "But he's guilty as all get out."

Jack turned to Rusty. "Why do you say that?"

"Because he keeps breaking my security cameras. I have him right on tape doing it. That kid is hiding something," Rusty said.

Jack sighed. "Do you want to press charges?"

"Nah." Rusty waved his hand through the air. "Ain't worth the paperwork. But I'm still keeping an eye on him."

Rachel said goodbye to Rusty and walked back to her car with Jack.

"That guy's a strange one, isn't he?" Jack asked, nodding toward Rusty's boat.

She chuckled. "He's a character, that's for sure. But he may be a good source of information."

"Maybe."

When they reached Rachel's car, she spoke up. "I'm beginning to think Adrian doesn't know anything. He really did look like he'd been out drowning his sorrows in alcohol. And he looked sad. I think he's taking Ariel's death badly."

"I don't know," Jack said. "But I'm not marking him off the suspect list quite yet." His expression softened. "So. How about dinner tonight? We can eat anywhere but here.'

Rachel hesitated. She would enjoy the company, but she didn't want to lead Jack to believe she was single. She finally decided to hit him with the truth. "I'd love to go to dinner, but I should tell you something. I'm in a relationship with another man."

"Oh." Jack looked thoughtful. "I didn't know. But you still have to eat, right?" He grinned.

She smiled. "Yes, I do. I just wanted to make sure you knew it was all business."

"I'll pick you up at seven," he said. "In the hotel lobby, if that's okay."

"That'll be fine. See you then." Rachel got into her car and drove off.

* * *

Rachel spent some time in her room answering emails from her clients. Afterward, she took a long walk on the beach. As she enjoyed the cool breeze off the Gulf, she thought about everything that had occurred over the past couple of weeks. When Rachel had first accepted the case from Ariel, she hadn't thought it was true. A dead ex-husband stalking Ariel? It had seemed too far-fetched to believe. Rachel had marked it down to exhaustion or nerves on Ariel's part. But Rachel hadn't thought it would hurt to investigate it to ease her friend's nerves. Now, Rachel realized she'd been wrong. Someone had been stalking Ariel—someone deadly. Maybe it hadn't been Randall, but it was someone who wanted Ariel's money and would do anything to get it. But who?

Adrian no longer seemed like a viable suspect to her. He'd looked devastated that Ariel had died. It just didn't seem plausible that he would have been the one to try to scare Ariel, let alone kill her.

So, who did?

She pondered this as she cleaned up and dressed for dinner. Rachel wasn't sure where Jack was taking her, so she put on a casual summer dress and low heels, then went down to the lobby to meet him. Jack showed up right on time.

"You look great," he said, smiling at her.

"Thanks." He'd worn cotton slacks and a shirt with a casual blazer over it, looking much more relaxed than he did in his dark work suit.

"I hope you aren't tired of seafood," he said as they walked out to his car.

She laughed. "Are you kidding? I could never get tired of seafood."

He drove up the coast to a restaurant that sat overlooking

the ocean. It was one of those great places that locals knew about, and tourists rarely went to.

"This looks nice," Rachel said as they were seated at a table with a view of the water. They ordered drinks and the waitress left them to look over the menu.

"This is one of my favorite restaurants when I want a quiet place to take someone," Jack said, setting the menu aside.

Rachel's brows rose. "As in when you go out on a date?"

He grinned. "Sometimes. Or when I take a friend out."

She nodded, thankful Jack understood this wasn't a date. Once their drinks came, they ordered dinner, and then Rachel spoke up. "I've been thinking a lot about this crazy case. There are so many things that don't make sense." She pulled a small notebook out of her purse. "So I wrote down a few things—a timeline of sorts—and I thought we could go over everything piece by piece. Maybe we're missing something."

Jack laughed. "Great minds think alike. I was thinking the exact same thing." He pulled a notepad out of his jacket pocket and showed it to her. "Let's wait until after dinner to compare notes, though. For once, I'd like to enjoy a meal that wasn't work-related."

She set her notepad aside. "Okay. What would you like to talk about?"

"Tell me what you do when you aren't sleuthing," he said. "You told me before you design book covers. That sounds like an interesting job."

"It is. That's how I know, well, knew Ariel. I've been designing covers for her for about four years. I have several regular clients and then new ones all the time. It's fun working with the various authors."

"That's amazing. I've never thought of that as a freelance

job. I guess I always assumed designers work for publishers," Jack said.

"In some instances, they do, but it's becoming more of a freelance position. I work with self-published authors, and I work for a few publishers. Working at home was the perfect option for me, especially when my daughter was younger," Rachel said.

"It was nice meeting your daughter. You're lucky to have such a great relationship with her," he said. "My sister barely spoke to my mother when she was that age."

Rachel smiled. "I feel lucky too, although I've always tried to treat her like her own person instead of an extension of me. I think that's where parents have trouble—realizing their children have their own minds as they get older. Jules is smart. I trust her to make good decisions."

Their meals came—steak and lobster for him, shrimp scampi for her—and as they ate, they continued talking about their lives. It was a nice break from discussing the case.

"Tell me how you decided to work in law enforcement," Rachel said. "I'm always intrigued why someone chooses that profession when it's not safe or rarely appreciated."

Jack looked thoughtful. "I went in the service for four years after high school, and I just kind of gravitated to law enforcement when I got out. I went to college and studied criminal justice, not sure how I would use my degree. I could have gone into social work or even on to be a lawyer, but I decided working homicides would be fun." He grinned mischievously, making her laugh. "But honestly, I like serving the community by getting criminals off the street. It may not always be popular, but I'm doing the best job I can to protect people. And I get to meet interesting people like you." He winked.

Rachel felt heat rise up into her face. She couldn't believe he'd made her blush. Jack had such a casual, off-handed way about him that made her feel comfortable with him. Maybe too comfortable.

"Is that how you get the criminals to confess? By charming them?" she teased.

"Any way I can," he said.

They finished their meal, and Rachel ordered a Coke instead of another glass of wine to keep her head clear. It was too easy to get pulled into Jack's flirting, and she wanted to be all business when they discussed the Weathers's case.

"Okay," Jack said, opening his own notebook after sipping his second beer. "I think we should write down what we both know and see what we come up with. There must be something in our notes that together we can figure this case out."

Rachel opened her own notepad, thankful that Jack was all business now. It would be hard to work alongside him on this case if their relationship turned awkward.

They went over the timeline of Randall's death and when the body part was found that identified him. Then they made a list of all the people Jack had interviewed about the case and who Rachel had interviewed.

"Did you think it was odd that Ariel supplied the DNA sample to identify Randall's leg?" Rachel asked. "I mean, who keeps their ex-husband's hairbrush around after the divorce?"

"Interesting question," Jack said, tapping his pen on the notepad. "At the time, I didn't really put much thought into it. Some people are slow to clean things out. But, as you say, why would she still have it?"

"Unless," Rachel said.

"Unless what?"

"Unless he was still coming to the house to spend the night after their divorce, so he needed some personal items there." She rose her brows, unsure of what Jack would think of this. Was she overthinking?

"Hm. Another good thought. Do you think the divorce was for reasons other than a bad marriage?" he asked.

She shrugged. "Ariel said they were happy until she started earning a higher income. Then Randall suddenly turned into a playboy and was sleeping with young girls. But would that really happen? Especially since he was already deep into embezzling money from his workplace. There had to be something more to it."

"Like them both getting greedy and wanting the life insurance money?" Jack asked.

"It could be. Or he was protecting their assets in case he was caught and charged for embezzlement. He ended up lucky by only being fired," Rachel said.

"They sound like a greedy couple," Jack said, looking disgusted. "They both could have been in on his faking his death for the money."

"Then why kill Ariel?" Rachel asked.

Jack sat back and took another sip of his beer. "I don't know. Maybe Randall became selfish and decided he wanted it all for himself. Or whoever was in on it with Ariel—because there's still a chance Randall is dead, and someone else killed Ariel."

"If Ariel was in on it, why would she ask me to look into it?" Rachel asked.

Jack sighed. "That's also a good question. Maybe she wanted someone else to know that she thought Randall was still alive in case something happened to her."

They discussed a few more details they each knew, which

reminded Rachel about something else Jack didn't have in his notes.

"What about the homeless man?"

His thick brows shot up. "Homeless man? Who's he?"

"He's the reason Rusty put up a camera on his boat. He'd been hanging around the marina for a while. He was also on the video Rusty gave me of the night before Randall supposedly died. Randall had a big party on his boat late that night, and everyone left the yacht except Randall and the homeless man."

"You have video?" Jack asked.

"Yes."

"Why is this the first time I've heard of it?"

"I guess it never came up with everything else that's happened," Rachel said. She dug in her purse and found the thumb drive she'd placed in there earlier in case Jack wanted a copy. She handed it to him. "I thought it was odd that a snob like Randall would invite a homeless man to party with them. Then I watched the entire thing and saw the man never left. The man who said he was Randall at my house said the homeless man was really a paid hitman out to get him. But I have other ideas about him."

"Such as?" Jack asked, looking intrigued.

"Maybe it was his body part that showed up floating in the gulf," Rachel said.

Jack sat back. "Wow. Either you have a really good imagination, or you're on to something." He stared at her a moment, then broke out laughing. She joined in. "This case is completely crazy."

"It is," she agreed.

"I'm going to Ariel's house tomorrow to speak with her

sister," Jack said. "I want to look over the scene again and see if Alivia knows more than she's saying."

"That's a tough one," Rachel said. "You don't want to upset her since her sister died, but what if she's involved? That would be awful."

"What do you know about Alivia?" Jack asked, looking serious again. "I can't seem to get a handle on her."

Rachel shook her head. "Absolutely nothing. She seems like the quiet, shy type. Ariel made a few comments about having to take care of her sister like she resented it. Alivia worked as her assistant and lived on the property. Other than that, I don't know anything."

Jack nodded and was about to say something else when Rachel's phone buzzed.

She glanced at it and smiled. "Sorry. I didn't realize it was already ten o'clock. The guy I'm seeing always texts me around this time." She quickly texted him back and then put her phone down again.

"Well, I guess that's my cue." Jack looked disappointed. "I'd better take you back to your hotel before the boyfriend gets jealous."

"No worries. He's not like that," she said.

Jack paid the bill and drove her back to the hotel. "I'll call you after I talk with Alivia. Are you staying here a while or leaving tomorrow?"

"I think I'll stay at least another night," Rachel said. "I'm interested in what you learn tomorrow."

"Okay. Good." Jack hesitated. "I had fun tonight, even if we were only discussing the case. It's been a long time since I've been able to toss ideas around with someone else, other than co-workers."

"I enjoyed it too," Rachel said. "This is a complicated case. Or a mess—I haven't decided which." They both laughed. "Oh, by the way. Did you get any footage from Ariel's house? She has cameras all over there."

"I asked Alivia for it, but she stalled and said she'd give it to me tomorrow. We didn't have a reason for a warrant to take any electronic devices, unfortunately. Hopefully, she gives me something I can use."

"You might want to ask her about the Bahama house, too," Rachel said offhandedly.

"Wait? What? What Bahama house?" Jack asked.

Rachel crossed her arms, feeling uncomfortable about sharing this information now that Ariel was dead. "I figured you didn't know about it. Ariel bought it to spend time down in the Bahamas. But honestly, after everything that's happened, I think she was planning on going down there and not returning."

CHAPTER THIRTEEN

Jack's mouth dropped open as he stared at Rachel. "How do you know about a house in the Bahamas and I don't?"

Rachel shrugged. "I forgot to mention it. There's just so much going on. The first day I met with Ariel, I saw paperwork for the purchase on her desk. She explained she wanted to have it as a vacation home. I didn't think much about it until I started thinking that she and Randall might be in on the faked death together. Maybe she and Randall—or whoever was involved—were going to go away for good."

Jack shook his head. "Are you sure you aren't a professional investigator? You've picked up on so much more than I have. I feel like I'm losing my touch."

Rachel chuckled. "I'm sure you aren't. I just happened to be in the right place at the right time."

"Well, I have a lot to look into tomorrow. Thank you for all your help. I'll call you tomorrow."

They said goodbye, and Rachel went up to her room. She couldn't help but like Jack. He was a nice guy who wasn't jaded yet by how he made a living. Her phone buzzed as she was changing for bed, and she realized she hadn't checked for another message from Avery yet.

"Are you out on the town with that Lieutenant and have forgotten all about poor little me all alone at home?" Jack had texted.

Rachel smiled. He was such a clown sometimes. *"Yes. We went dining and dancing and had a great old time."*

"Really?"

"Gotcha! We only had dinner and talked about murder all evening. Does that make you feel better?" Rachel texted.

"A little. All kidding aside, I hope you're safe there. No dead guys bothering you?" Avery texted.

"No. Only live guys."

"Well, that doesn't make me feel any better," Avery texted. *"Keep me posted. Goodnight."*

"I will. Goodnight." Rachel set her phone down. She missed Avery already.

* * *

The next morning Rachel went for a long walk on the beach and let her mind wander through all the information she had on Ariel's case. Nothing new came to her, though. She was eager to hear what Jack learned from Alivia.

Rachel spent the rest of the morning working on a couple of projects. She'd set up her computer outside on the patio to enjoy the beautiful weather and scenery. She ordered lunch from the hotel and sat outside to eat it. When her phone buzzed at one o'clock, she thought it would be Jack, but was surprised when she answered to find it was Rusty.

"Hey there, little lady," Rusty said. "I hope I'm not bothering you."

"Not at all," she told him. "Is something wrong?"

"I think something's up over at pretty boy's yacht. He's hauled several armloads of supplies from his car—like groceries and stuff. I think he's planning on skipping town."

Rachel remembered Jack telling Adrian not to go anywhere. "Thanks for letting me know," she told Rusty. "I'll tell Jack right away. He'll want to know this."

"Good. I don't want that guy getting away with anything. By the way, remember when I said there was a blond gal at Adrian's over Thanksgiving weekend?" Rusty asked.

"Yeah. Why?" Rachel couldn't figure out why Rusty would bring that up.

"Well, I was right. She wasn't a redhead; she was blond. Her hair was short, like above the shoulders. Definitely not red, though."

Rachel frowned. How could that be if Alivia was the one who spent time on the boat with Adrian? "Thanks, Rusty. I'll pass that along to Jack too."

"Okay, little lady. I'll talk to you later." Rusty hung up.

Rachel was anxious to tell Jack what she'd learned but didn't want to disturb him if he was still at Alivia's. Still, if Adrian was making a run for it, Jack had to know. She decided to text him instead of calling.

"Rusty just told me that Adrian was stocking up his boat. Leaving town, maybe? Just thought you should know."

Her phone rang only seconds after sending the text. It was Jack.

"I just finished talking with Alivia. Can you meet me somewhere?"

"How about The Mermaid's Cove?" she said.

He chuckled. "I like how you think. I'll be there in a few minutes."

Rachel and Jack drove up at the same time, and they went immediately to an outdoor table and ordered drinks. From their vantage point, they could easily see if Adrian was stocking up his boat.

"I can't get another search warrant for Adrian's yacht, but there's no law against talking to him," Jack said. "We can watch for him while we talk."

"How did it go with Alivia?" Rachel asked.

"Interesting. I pushed her to give me an exact timeline when she came home and found her sister in the pool. She was vague, constantly changing the subject, which I found suspicious. Why would she hesitate like that? Anyway, she said she left Adrian's around noon, stopped at a couple of stores, then picked up groceries before arriving home somewhere around two."

"Has the coroner come up with a time of death yet?" Rachel asked.

Jack grinned. "Good question. It hasn't been made public yet, but Ariel died sometime around noon. And there were remnants of sleeping pills and alcohol in her system."

Rachel frowned. "So, if Alivia came home after two o'clock, she couldn't have been there when Ariel drowned."

"You seem disappointed," Jack said.

"I'm just trying to figure this out," Rachel said. "I hadn't thought Alivia was involved, but now that I know she's been seeing Adrian, there's a possibility. Except for one thing—Rusty's camera caught a blond woman going to Adrian's for the weekend. Not a redhead."

Jack stared at her, stunned. "Wait. So, was it Alivia or Ariel who spent the weekend?"

"I don't know. From a distance, they look so much alike.

But Alivia is definitely not blond."

Jack sat back, contemplating this. "Rusty has video?"

"He says he does."

"Then it makes sense that Adrian wanted to destroy Rusty's cameras and the one here at the Cove. Could Alivia have murdered Ariel out of jealousy?" Jack asked.

Rachel shook her head. "I don't know." She looked up and pointed toward the marina. "There's Adrian now. He's carrying some more bags to his boat."

"I think we should pay him a visit." Jack stood up and tossed money on the table. "Let's go."

Rachel followed him down to the dock. "Did you get any video from Ariel's surveillance cameras?"

Jack threw her a wry grin. "You'll never guess. They weren't running at the time. There's nothing on them."

"Do you believe that?"

"Not on your life. I'm sure someone erased them. I have no idea who at this point."

They reached Adrian's boat just as he was coming up from below. Jack had Rachel stay on the dock while he stepped on deck.

"What do you want?" Adrian said, scowling at them.

"I heard you've been stocking up on supplies. Are you taking a trip?" Jack asked.

"I don't have to tell you anything," Adrian said. "I'm free to do whatever I want."

"We're in the middle of a murder investigation here," Jack said. "I told you not to leave town."

Adrian blanched. "I thought Ariel's death was an accident. Are you telling me someone murdered her?"

"That's what we're trying to figure out."

Adrian's face hardened. "You can either arrest me or leave me alone. You can't stop me from leaving."

Rachel moved closer to the boat and spoke in a gentle voice. "Adrian? I don't believe you did anything wrong. What are you running away from? What's scaring you?"

He turned his eyes in her direction, and suddenly his angry expression crumpled. Adrian sat heavily on the bench seat. "I can't believe anyone would hurt Ariel. I don't want to stick around and be next."

Jack turned to Rachel and waved her onto the boat. She approached Adrian and sat down beside him. "Adrian. If you know anything about Randall or Ariel's deaths, you need to tell us. You won't be safe until you do."

He raised his eyes to Rachel's. "I don't know anything. I loved Ariel. I would have done anything for her. I can't believe anyone would hurt her."

"I was just trying to help Ariel, too," Rachel said. "And a strange man came to my house to scare me. So, I get why you're afraid."

Adrian's eyes widened. "Was it Randall?" he asked.

"He said he was Randall."

His jaw tightened. "I can't help you with anything. It's putting my life at risk."

She placed her hand on his arm to calm him. "I understand. Can I ask you one more question?"

He nodded.

"A blond woman was seen coming and going from your boat the same weekend as Alivia was supposed to be here. Was it Ariel?"

Adrian looked confused a moment, then shook his head. "No. It was Alivia. Ariel had talked her into dying her hair blond to confuse the man following her."

"But Alivia's hair was red when we went to her house on Sunday after she'd found her sister in the pool," Jack interjected.

"Oh. I suppose she'd washed it out before that. It was one of those non-permanent dyes. Alivia told me that she'd put away the groceries and took a shower before walking to the guest house. That's when she saw Ariel in the pool."

Rachel and Jack exchanged a look. "Why didn't she shower at your place?" Rachel asked.

"She hates my shower. She says I'm a terrible housekeeper, and she's right," Adrian said.

"Will you do me a favor, please?" Jack said. "Stay around town until we figure this out. Otherwise, you'll look guilty. I'm with Rachel. I don't believe you've done anything wrong. But it won't look that way if you take off."

Adrian nodded. "Fine. I'll stay put." His eyes rose to Jack. "But find the person who killed Ariel. Because she didn't deserve to die that way."

"I'm trying. Believe me," Jack said.

Once Rachel and Jack were in the parking lot, he spoke up. "What do you think?"

"I think he's just as confused as we are. Maybe he knows something, but now things have turned on him. This is no longer a crazy case. Things are getting scary," Rachel said.

Jack nodded. "I agree. I'll follow you back to your hotel to ensure you're safe, then I'm going to headquarters. Are you staying another night or driving home?"

"I think I'll stay another night. Why don't you drop by the hotel tonight, and we can eat there and talk some more," Rachel said.

Jack grinned. "I never say no to dinner with a pretty woman."

She rolled her eyes, and they took off in their separate cars.

Once in her hotel room, Rachel sat down with her notepad and began going over the Weathers's case again. There were so many twists and turns that it was hard to settle on just one scenario. The idea that Alivia could have had anything to do with Ariel's murder was unsettling. A sister, especially a twin sister, killing her twin over jealousy or money was hard for Rachel to fathom. But Alivia could be completely innocent too. Even thinking she could be guilty bothered Rachel. After all, Alivia had just lost her sister—the woman who supported her and cared for her.

Rachel looked over her list again.

— Randall Weathers died in a boating accident. A leg was found in the water and identified as his.
— Ariel had been the one to supply the DNA sample.
— Randall had a party the night before he died and invited a homeless man that Adrian claimed had fixed the boat engine.
— There was video of Adrian going over to Randall's boat for about an hour that morning before the boat blew up. There was no sign of the homeless man leaving.
— Adrian followed Randall's boat out to the Gulf in time to see it engulfed in flames.
— Months later, Ariel contacted her, stating her dead ex-husband was stalking her.
— A man who claimed to be Randall came to Rachel's house and told her Ariel had hired a hitman to kill him, so he faked his death and now wanted half the life insurance money.

— Ariel told Rachel that she'd take care of it and then ended up dead the following Sunday.

— Alivia had spent Thanksgiving weekend on Adrian's boat and went home to find Ariel in the pool.

— Adrian claimed that Alivia had dyed her hair blond to confuse the man following Ariel around.

Rachel stared at these facts until her head ached. Everyone seemed guilty. It still made no sense. If Ariel knew Randall had faked his death for the insurance money, then why would Ariel hire her to look into it? Everyone—Adrian, Alivia, and even Rachel—seemed to be a fall guy for some crazy scheme. But what had that plan been?

Staring at the list, a thought struck her. If Ariel knew Randall had faked his death and they were going to run away with the insurance money, what would happen to the money now that she was dead?

And who inherits Ariel's two-million-dollar life insurance policy?

CHAPTER FOURTEEN

Rachel met Jack at the hotel's outdoor patio restaurant at six that evening. She had her list in hand and couldn't wait to talk to him.

"Did you learn anything new since we spoke?" Rachel asked after they'd ordered drinks.

Looking tired, Jack said, "The coroner is going to officially mark her death as accidental. There were no marks on her body and no sign of a struggle. So, this throws a big curveball in the case. No murder, no case."

Rachel's mouth dropped open. She hadn't expected this. "What about her stalker? You reported that a man had been in her backyard. Isn't that enough to keep the case open?"

He took a long drink of his beer, then ran his hand over his short hair. "Not according to my superiors. Ariel had been drinking, had sleeping pills still in her system, and fell into the pool. End of story."

Rachel deflated. She sat back in her chair and stared out toward the ocean. The sun had already gone down, but she could hear the waves as they hit the shore. It should have been soothing, but she was too upset by this turn of events to feel calm. "So, that's it?"

He nodded. "That's it. Unless you can come up with something spectacular."

The waitress came and took their order. Rachel ordered grilled chicken and a salad, but her appetite had waned. After the waitress left, she leaned in closer toward Jack. "Someone is going to get away with murder."

"I agree," Jack said. "But who? There are so many suspects, yet not one we can pin it on. And I'd be hung out to dry if I told my boss that I thought Randall was still alive and he killed his ex-wife. That would be the end of my career."

Rachel closed her notebook. "Then I guess we have no need to discuss this anymore."

Jack looked up at her with interest. "Did you come up with anything new?"

"Only a question I hadn't thought of before," she said.

"What?"

She looked up into his eyes. "If Ariel is dead and Randall is dead, who inherits all the money? Ariel also had a two-million-dollar life insurance policy on her."

Jack's brows rose. "Really? How do you know that?"

"Ariel told me the first time I went to her house. She said both she and Randall had life insurance policies on them. She inherited Randall's, but who inherits hers?"

Jack's eyes lit up. "You just may have given me enough to keep this case open—a motive for murder. First thing tomorrow, I'm calling Alivia to ask her who gets the money. Great job, Rachel."

She could feel her face heat up in a blush. "Thanks. I guess I thought you would have asked her who inherited everything."

He grimaced. "I was so busy trying to find leads to prove

it was a murder that I hadn't thought about the money. I just assumed Alivia would inherit everything. And if that's the case, then I have more investigating to do."

"Then I'm glad I brought it up." She grinned at him.

Their meals came, and Jack lifted his beer glass in a toast. "To solving cases," he said.

Rachel laughed and clinked her Coke glass with his. "To solving cases."

They sat there a moment in comfortable silence, each in their own thoughts. Rachel spoke first. "If the coroner is finished with his investigation, then I suppose Ariel's body will be released to the family soon."

"Yes. That could mean the funeral will be soon," Jack said. "Will you be attending it?"

"If Alivia makes it a public event, I will," she said. "So, I suppose I should go home tomorrow and get some work done. Then I'll come back for the funeral."

"That's a shame," Jack said, looking disappointed. "Who will I bounce case ideas off of? Who will I eat all my meals with?"

She laughed. "You can call me if anything interesting comes up. And I'm sure there are plenty of beautiful women who'd enjoy dining with you."

"You'd think, wouldn't you?" he winked. "Unfortunately, I don't have time to meet interesting women with the hours I keep." His expression turned serious. "At least not ones as interesting as you."

Rachel was speechless. She hadn't expected their banter to turn serious.

"I've embarrassed you," Jack said. "I'm sorry. I don't want to make things awkward. It's just that I'll miss your company."

"I'll miss yours too," she said.

Their food came, and they both ate in silence for a time. Jack looked up from his steak dinner and grinned his usual mischievous grin. The same grin that Rachel had initially thought was arrogant and cocky but now knew he wore when he teased.

"So, where is that man of yours? Doesn't it drive him crazy not being with you?" Jack asked.

Rachel laughed. "I'm sure he can hardly stand being away. Avery lives in Baltimore where his work is. But we try to see each other whenever we can."

"Ah. A long-distance relationship. Interesting," Jack cocked an eyebrow. "How did you two meet?"

"He helped me with the case in California about the girl in the grave," she said. "He was investigating the murder of his mother, which happened around the same time as the little girl's murder. We figured it out together."

Jack's face wrinkled, looking deep in thought. "The FBI guy who helped you solve the case?"

It surprised Rachel that Jack knew this. "Yes. We grew close working together."

"I can understand how that can happen," Jack said.

Rachel dropped her eyes to her food.

"Sorry, again," he said.

They finished their dinner, and Jack walked into the lobby with Rachel.

"I'll call you if anything else comes up. Otherwise, maybe I'll see you at Ariel's funeral," Jack said hopefully.

"I'll be there." She stood there feeling awkward, then laughed.

"What's so funny?" Jack asked.

"I feel like I should be thanking you for something, but I

have no idea what for," Rachel said.

Jack bent down and gently kissed her cheek. "You're welcome." He gave her that cocky grin, winked, and headed out the door.

Rachel shook her head and walked to her room. Jack Meyers was a self-assured, arrogant guy. Yet, she couldn't help but like him.

* * *

Thursday morning, Rachel drove back to her home in Talla-hassee. She had a pile of emails to answer and projects to work on. She knew she should call Jules to catch her up on the case and visit her Aunt Julie at the memory care unit. It was the first week in December, and even though the weather didn't feel like it, Christmas was coming up fast, and she had shopping to do. Yet all Rachel could think about was the Weathers's case.

Early Friday morning, she visited her Aunt Julie and then bought some groceries before returning home. By afternoon, she was deep into her work when her phone buzzed. She answered quickly when she saw it was Jack.

"Hello. Are you already missing me?" Rachel teased.

"Absolutely," he answered lightly. Then his tone turned serious. "I went to see Alivia, but she refused to talk to me. She said she'd had enough of being questioned by the police, and since Ariel's death was officially an accident, she wasn't required to talk to me. Unfortunately, she's correct. I have no power anymore to make her talk. So, I didn't learn whether or not she'd inherited all the money."

This surprised Rachel. "Your captain didn't think it was a motive for murder?"

"My captain says there is no murder, so therefore, no motive. He handed me a bunch of new files and said to move on to other cases."

Rachel sighed. "That's a shame. Two people are dead, and no one cares why."

"I'm sorry, Rachel," Jack said, sounding disappointed. "We did our best."

"I guess that's it then," she said. "Will you still be going to the funeral?"

"I definitely will. Who knows? Maybe Randall will show up in one of his crazy disguises, and we can prove we were right."

She laughed. "That would be a sight—you running after a dead man, knocking down mourners at the funeral."

"Surprisingly, it wouldn't be the first time." He chuckled.

After she'd hung up, disappointment enveloped Rachel. Something wasn't right with the whole case. Who was the man who'd scared her here at her house? And who was the Randall impersonator at Ariel's house? Those things happened. Yet, she had no idea who the culprit was.

That evening, Rachel ran everything past Jules when they met for dinner. The younger woman thought about what Rachel had told her as she ate her pasta.

"It's strange that they don't want to investigate who'd been stalking Ariel," Jules finally said. "When someone complains they're being followed and ends up dead, it seems obvious they might have been murdered."

"Right?" Rachel said. "Even though there were no marks on Ariel's body, it doesn't mean someone didn't push her into the pool. Since she had sleeping pills in her system and had been drinking, she could have drowned without force. The question is, who? The guy who said he was Randall told me he didn't want to hurt Ariel."

"Maybe Ariel refused to give him any of the money," Jules said.

Rachel took a sip of her drink. "Killing her wouldn't have gotten him the money either. Randall's supposed to be dead. How could he withdraw the money?"

Jules shook her head. "It was an odd case, Mom. To tell the truth, I'm glad you aren't involved anymore. It became dangerous when the stalker set his sights on you."

"Yeah. I'm not cut out for all this cloak and dagger stuff," Rachel said. "The next time someone asks me to help them solve a case, I'm saying no. And if I don't say no, then please smack me to remind me."

Jules laughed. "Yeah. Like you'd listen to me."

That night, as Rachel got into bed, she turned on the television to find a comedy to watch. She was surprised to see a news channel talking about Ariel Weathers.

"The funeral of author Ariel Weathers has been set for next Friday," the newswoman stated. *"Her sister, Alivia Hanson, is opening it up to the public because so many of Ariel's fans wanted to attend the services. Ariel's death was pronounced an accident by the county coroner late yesterday. As you may remember, Ariel's ex-husband, Randall Weathers, died in a boating accident several months before."*

A chill ran through Rachel as she watched a photo of Ariel pop up on the screen. She was dressed in her usual colorful style with her bangles and many necklaces. Ariel shouldn't be dead. There was no reason for it. But there was nothing Rachel could do to prove she'd been murdered.

With a sigh, she turned off the television and lay down to sleep.

CHAPTER FIFTEEN

Rachel spent the next week working on projects for clients and making lists of everything she had to do before Christmas. She knew this year she wouldn't be able to bring Aunt Julie home for Christmas Eve, so she was trying to think of ways to make Julie's room feel festive. She and Jules would go the night before Christmas Eve to eat dinner with Julie, even though her aunt probably wouldn't recognize either of them. Then they could spend Christmas Eve at home, hopefully with Avery there for a few days.

Avery surprised her with a call that weekend.

"I just got approved to take time off over Christmas," he said, sounding excited. "Do you think you can stand to have me there the twenty-third through New Year's?"

Rachel was ecstatic. "I'm sure I can work you into my schedule," she teased. "I'm so glad you're coming. After this hectic year, it will be fun to spend some downtime with you."

"I agree," he said. "I saw on the news that Ariel's funeral is next Friday. Are you still planning on going?"

"I am," Rachel said. "I feel like that's the least I can do. She asked me to look into her stalker, and she ended up dead."

"It wasn't your fault, Rachel," Avery said. "You warned her that it could be dangerous meeting with Randall or whoever was blackmailing her. She chose not to listen. You did what you could."

"I know," she said. "I'm also going to give Alivia the check back that Ariel had given me. There's no way I can take her money. But I'll wait a few days after the funeral to do that."

"Well, be careful. You aren't certain that Alivia wasn't involved in Ariel's death. Can't you just mail it to her?"

"No. I really should do it in person. Truthfully, I don't believe Alivia killed her sister. She was already being taken care of by Ariel, so why kill her for her money?"

Avery chuckled. "You have to learn to be more cynical—like me."

This made Rachel laugh. "Never!"

They talked a while longer and then hung up. Rachel was thrilled Avery was coming for Christmas. She couldn't wait to see him again.

* * *

On the day of the funeral, Jack called Rachel and asked if she'd like to meet at the police station and ride together. The funeral was being held outside in a lovely park by the ocean. "Parking is going to be murder," Jack told her.

"Great analogy," Rachel said.

"Sorry."

She agreed it was a good idea, and two hours later, she pulled up next to his car at the station.

"You look good," Jack said, smiling at her. "Serious, but good."

Rachel smiled back. She was wearing a black sleeveless dress and low heels and brought a cotton blazer to wear if the breeze off the Gulf was cold. "I'm old-fashioned," she told Jack. "I still believe in dressing respectfully at funerals."

"You mean like me?" He pretended to model his usual dark suit.

"Yes. Like you," she said.

They drove the short distance to the park, and as predicted, the parking was crazy. Jack made use of his police badge to park in a no-parking zone, and they made their way through the crowd to where the service was being held.

"There are a lot of people here," Jack commented, glancing around. "Do you think these are all friends or just curious onlookers?"

"I don't know. I know Ariel's books had a good-sized following. It could be fans."

"Do you mind if we sit near the back?" Jack asked. "It'll give me a better view of who's here."

"That's fine," Rachel said.

There were rows of chairs set up facing the ocean and a podium at the front for speakers. Rachel spotted Alivia, dressed all in black, in the front row. It looked like Adrian was next to her. She didn't recognize any of the other family members attending.

"Is that an urn up there behind the podium?" Rachel whispered to Jack. "Was Ariel cremated?"

Jack nodded. "Yes. If any more evidence was needed, it's all ashes now."

Rachel shook her head, disappointed. Alivia had the right to do whatever she wanted with Ariel's remains. Still, it always looked suspicious when a body from an investigation was cremated.

Finally, everyone settled into chairs, and a man dressed in a dark suit went to the podium. He spoke into the microphone, thanking everyone for attending.

"Ariel Weathers wasn't a religious person," the man said. "But she did believe in the spirit world and a higher power. She loved the outdoors, and especially the beach and ocean. She and her husband enjoyed being on the water in their boat and taking trips to the Bahamas. So, it only seemed natural to celebrate her life outside, by the water."

As the man continued to talk, Rachel scanned the mourners. She didn't see anyone who could be Randall, hiding among the crowd. She noticed that Adrian occasionally placed his arm around Alivia as she dabbed at her eyes with a tissue. Sitting so far behind them, though, made it hard to see everything.

"Do you see anyone suspicious?" Jack whispered to Rachel.

"No. Although there are a few colorful characters in the group," she said. Some women were dressed in bright, flowery clothing and draped in jewelry, an odd look for a funeral. "They must be fans of Ariel's."

"That's what I was thinking," Jack said.

After the man speaking had covered the main points of Ariel's life, he invited Alivia to come up and say a few words. Rachel watched intently as Alivia walked up to the podium in tall heels. When she turned to face the crowd, Rachel was surprised to see that her hat had black netting attached that covered half of her face. It looked old-fashioned for Alivia, who usually dressed casually.

"Thank you all for attending my dear sister's funeral," Alivia said into the microphone. "She would be thrilled to see so many people gathered here just for her." As she spoke, Rachel noticed she kept dabbing at her eyes with a tissue, careful not

to smudge her makeup. Rachel thought that was odd. Whenever she'd seen Alivia at the house, the woman had worn little
to no makeup.

As Alivia moved while she spoke, the sun sparkled off the
many gold chains she wore. She spoke of how much Ariel had
loved her career as a writer and how thankful she'd been to
have so many loyal fans. Her speech was a very moving tribute
to her sister's life.

"I always had the impression Alivia was shy," Jack said to
Rachel. "Maybe I was wrong."

"I thought that too," Rachel told him.

After Alivia spoke, the man in the dark suit came back
to the podium. "I'm sure you all understand how traumatic
this loss has been for Ariel's family, so they will not be greet-
ing everyone after the service. But they encourage everyone to
linger a while and take this opportunity to share stories with
each other about Ariel's life." With that, he ended the service
with a short, non-denominational prayer.

"I was hoping to have a chance to give my condolences to
Alivia," Rachel said. "I guess I'll have to wait until another time."

"I can't blame her, though. Reception lines after a funeral
are hard," Jack said.

Rachel nodded. Everyone around them rose, and people
were mingling around the park. Bottles of water and soda were
on a table on one side, along with plates of cookies and other
treats.

"What now?" Rachel asked as they made their way through
the crowd.

"I'd really like to wander a few minutes and get a good
look at everyone," Jack said. "Can I meet you back here in a
few minutes?"

"Sure. That's fine."

Jack walked away, and Rachel walked over to the table of refreshments. She picked up a water bottle and moved away from the crowd, closer toward the ocean view. Rachel stood there, enjoying the breeze and watching as the waves tumbled onto shore. Rachel thought about Alivia and how she'd looked today in the black dress and old-style hat. Something about it looked off. Her idea of Alivia was of a woman who loved jean shorts, tank tops, and an easy lifestyle. Basically, the exact opposite of Ariel. So why did she seem so different today?

"What are you doing here?" a deep voice said directly behind her. Rachel startled and spun around. She knew that voice. It sounded like the same voice she'd heard that night at her house. The night Randall had scared her. But it wasn't Randall standing there when she turned. It was Adrian.

"You scared me," she said, relieved she knew who it was.

"Sorry," Adrian said, running his hand over his head and then stopping midway. "I'm just surprised to see you here."

Rachel stood her ground. "Why? I was Ariel's friend. She asked me to look into the whole Randall-has-come-back-from-the-dead mystery. Why shouldn't I be here?"

"Oh, right," Adrian said. He squinted at her. "You're not still looking into that, are you? They're gone—both of them. Just leave it be."

"No. I'm not looking into it anymore," Rachel said, her tone softer. "I'm sorry you lost your friends. I know how close you were to Randall and Ariel."

"Thank you," Adrian said.

Jack walked up then, and Adrian frowned. "You shouldn't be here. You upset Alivia the last time you went to her house."

"I'm just paying my respects, that's all," Jack said. "I

wouldn't dream of upsetting Alivia again."

Adrian gave a curt nod and stalked off.

"Sheesh. What was that all about?" Jack asked Rachel.

She sighed. "I think he's hurting. He really did care for Randall and Ariel. But he scared the bejesus out of me." She looked directly at Jack. "When he came up behind me, he sounded just like the man who'd come to my house."

Jack's face creased with concern. "It could have been him."

"Maybe. But why?"

"That's the question that keeps coming up in this whole case," Jack said, sounding disgusted. "Why? And until I can find out why any of it happened, there is no case."

"I'm sorry," Rachel said, placing a comforting hand on his arm.

He grinned. "Thanks. Are you ready to leave?"

"Absolutely."

"Can I buy you lunch before you head home?" he asked as they walked to his car.

"That would be great. I'm starved."

He took her to a little place not far from the park where they could sit on a deck overlooking the ocean. Rachel ordered a shrimp salad, and Jack had a hamburger and fries. She laughed after the waitress left the table.

"How do you keep in shape when you eat so much greasy food?" she asked.

His brows shot up. "You think I'm in good shape?"

She felt her face burn with embarrassment. "It's not like I'm looking or anything," she said. "But it's obvious you're not overweight."

He chuckled. "I was just teasing you. It's easy to make you blush, you know that?"

Rachel rolled her eyes. "I'll bet you work out all the time. You probably take your dog, Captain, out running on the beach every morning and then hit the gym at night."

Jack grinned. "I do run with my dog a couple of times a week. But no gym. I have my own workout equipment at home." He winked at her.

"Then I was half right," she said.

Their food came, and their conversation turned back to Ariel and Randall.

"If Randall's plan was to pretend he's dead to get half of the life insurance money, then it makes no sense to kill Ariel," Jack said. "Unless he was afraid she'd tell the police so she could keep the money for herself."

"If Randall did fake his death and he killed Ariel," Rachel said. "Then he's still out there somewhere."

Jack was just about to eat a French fry when she said this. He set it down and stared at her. "You're right. Where do you think he'd be?"

She shrugged. "He could be anywhere. No one is looking for him. Their favorite spot was a certain island in the Bahamas. Maybe he's headed there."

"Or he may have bought a used boat he can escape to the Bahamas with. I should circulate his photo around to boat dealers in the area. Someone may know what name he's using now," Jack said, looking excited.

"That's a good idea," Rachel said. "But what will your superior think?"

"What he doesn't know won't hurt him," Jack said with a glint in his eye. "It's a long shot anyway, but worth a try."

After they'd eaten, Jack drove her back to her car at the station. They sat in his car a moment, and then Jack spoke up.

"So, I suppose this is the last time I'll see you."

"I suppose so," she said. "I doubt I'll be running into you in Tallahassee anytime soon."

"Yeah. I doubt that too." They got out of the car, and he walked her to hers.

"Well, I'll see you around," she said, smiling. It seemed strange to be saying goodbye forever to Jack. They'd spent so much time together; it was like losing a friend. She climbed behind the wheel as Jack held the door.

Taking a breath, Jack leaned on the door and looked down at Rachel. "I don't think it's a secret that I like you, so I'll just put it out there and never say another word about it. If Mr. FBI Guy ever forgets how lucky he is, I'll be here."

Rachel's heart jumped; she was stunned by his words. "I'll keep that in mind," she said.

He nodded, shut her door, and waited until she'd driven off down the road.

CHAPTER SIXTEEN

Before driving the two hours home, Rachel decided to stop at the marina and talk to Rusty. On the ride there, her head was spinning from Jack's last words to her. She'd come to like Jack a lot, despite initially thinking he was cocky and arrogant. He was a smart, handsome man who was dedicated to his job just like Avery was. But Rachel hadn't thought of Jack in a romantic way. She was in love with Avery, despite their long-distance relationship. Still, to have Jack say that was both a compliment and a complication.

Rachel brushed her personal problems aside as she parked at the marina and walked down to the dock. As she approached Rusty's boat, she glanced over at Adrian's. There was no movement there, and she figured he was at Alivia's house comforting her.

"Ahoy, there pretty lady," Rusty bellowed as she approached his boat. "My, but aren't you looking fancy today."

Rachel smiled—something about Rusty always lifted her spirits. "Permission to come aboard?" she asked playfully.

"Permission granted. Always," Rusty said, offering his hand to help her aboard. "What can I do for you today, little lady?"

"I just attended Ariel Weathers's funeral, and I started thinking about the video you said you had of a blond woman over at Adrian's Thanksgiving weekend."

"Ah, yes," Rusty said, running his hand through his long beard. "Did you want to see it? I kept a copy in case the police were interested."

"I was hoping you'd offer," Rachel said, grinning.

Rusty brought his laptop up on deck and found the video. Together, they watched several clips of Adrian and a slender woman with a blond bob arriving and leaving the boat. The woman never looked directly at the camera, but it was obvious it was either Alivia or Ariel. The problem was it was difficult to tell exactly which one.

"Can I get a copy of those videos?" Rachel asked. "Maybe if I watch them closely at home, I can distinguish who she is."

"Sure," Rusty said. He went below to get a thumb drive, and they picked the video clips she wanted saved. "Honestly, I thought it was Randall's wife. She looked and sounded like her. I didn't know at the time she had a twin sister."

"It's difficult to tell when it's not a closeup," Rachel said.

After they'd finished copying the files to the drive, Rusty cocked his head and stared at Rachel. "I guess this means you aren't finished investigating this case?" His eyes twinkled mischievously.

She chuckled. "I guess I'm not. Something still seems off to me. Or maybe I'm too stubborn to let it go."

"Stubbornness is a virtue," Rusty said.

She thanked him for his help and headed back to her car to drive home. Rachel thought about Ariel and Alivia nearly the entire way home. They were so much alike, and yet so different. Something about the fact that Alivia was supposed to be at

Adrian's boat that weekend bothered her. She just didn't know what it was.

* * *

Once Rachel was home, she caught up on her work and plans for Christmas. She visited her Aunt Julie at the care center and brought a small tree and decorations to make her room feel festive. Rachel was rewarded by seeing Julie excited for the first time in a long while. Julie helped decorate the tree, and her eyes sparkled with joy.

"That's the happiest I've seen your aunt in a long time," Shirley told Rachel. "It was so thoughtful of you to decorate her room."

"It's nice seeing her smile for a change," Rachel said. She told Shirley to plan for her and Jules to have dinner with Julie the day before Christmas Eve. "Unfortunately, we won't be able to bring her home this year."

"Well, you three can have a nice Christmas no matter when it is. The important part is being together," Shirley assured her.

Avery said he was getting eager for the Christmas holiday too. "I can't wait to see you and Jules again," he told her one night on the phone. "And a week of no work! It will be so nice."

Rachel couldn't wait too. But she had so much to do that the time sped by.

A week after Ariel's funeral, Rachel hopped back in her car and drove to Panama City again. She wanted to return Ariel's check to Alivia in person and also offer her condolences. Even though Rachel hadn't known Alivia as well as she'd known Ariel, she felt obligated to do this face to face.

As Rachel pulled up in front of Ariel's house, the first thing she saw was the large For Sale sign. Sadness crept over her. Ariel had loved her house. Although, Rachel understood why Alivia would want to sell—after all, her sister had died there.

When Rachel reached the front porch, she glanced up to where the camera was. To her surprise, there was no security camera. Considering a strange man had been showing up in their yard only a few weeks ago, Rachel thought it was odd Alivia would have taken down the camera.

Unless Alivia had no reason to be afraid anymore.

Rachel knocked on the door, and only seconds later, Alivia answered it.

"Oh, Rachel. What a surprise," she said, looking stunned.

"Hi, Alivia. I'm sorry to just drop in, but I wanted to speak with you a moment if that's okay." Alivia looked young and slender in jean shorts and a billowy flowered top. The magenta color of the top made her pale skin glow.

Alivia looked past Rachel and glanced around as if expecting someone else to be there with her. "Are you alone?"

"Yes. It's just me," Rachel said, thinking her question was strange.

"Oh. Well. Okay." Alivia opened the door wider and moved aside so Rachel could come inside. "I've been busy packing things up, so I don't have much time."

"I'll only be a few minutes," Rachel said, glancing around. There were boxes everywhere. It looked like the kitchen had been packed up already, and Alivia was working on the smaller items in the living room. "I see you have the house up for sale," Rachel said casually.

Alivia followed her into the living room. "Yes. After what happened, I just can't bear to live here anymore."

"I can certainly understand that," Rachel said. She looked

out the back patio windows and noticed the pool had been covered.

Alivia's eyes followed her gaze. "I never want to swim in that pool again, so I covered it."

Rachel turned and looked into Alivia's green eyes. "I understand that too. I didn't get a chance to speak to you at the funeral. I'm so sorry for your loss. Ariel was such a kind, vivacious person, and I know she'll be greatly missed. Especially by you, considering how close you two were."

Alivia's eyes dropped. "Thank you. That's very kind of you. I will miss my twin sister. We had our differences, but we loved each other fiercely."

Rachel noticed how long Alivia's lashes were—so long that they looked fake. And she was wearing a heavy coat of makeup. Maybe she was more like Ariel than Rachel had first thought.

Reaching in her purse, Rachel pulled out the check Ariel had given her that first day she'd visited here. "I wanted to return Ariel's check. I never felt comfortable taking the money from her in the first place, and now, well, it seems irreverent." She reached out to hand the check to Alivia.

Alivia shook her head. "Oh, no, dear. Please, keep it. Ariel wanted you to have it. You did a lot of work trying to help her, and I know you were in danger also. I couldn't possibly take it back."

Rachel was about to respond, but a phone began ringing in the other room.

"Oh, that's my phone," Alivia said, rushing off to the office. "I'll be right back," she called over her shoulder.

Rachel watched her run in her wedged Espadrilles to the office and heard her answer the phone. Something was bothering Rachel, but she just couldn't put her finger on it. Casually, she followed Alivia into the office, glancing at the bookshelf where she'd last seen photos of Ariel, Randall, Adrian, and Alivia on the boat. The photos, however, were gone.

"Yes, yes, I know. I'm working as fast as I can," Alivia said hastily into the phone. She'd turned away when she'd seen Rachel enter the room. "Everything will be done. Don't worry," she said quieter.

Rachel moved closer to the desk. Ariel's computer was sitting there as it had the last time Rachel was here. Next to it, lying on a pile of papers, looked like a printout of an airline receipt. Rachel studied it as best she could from a distance. It looked like two tickets had been purchased from Miami to Nassau, Bahamas, on the twenty-second of December.

"Those real estate agents can be so pushy," Alivia said when she clicked off the phone.

Rachel smiled and nodded, although she didn't believe Alivia had been talking to a real estate agent.

"I hate to be rude, but was there anything else, dear?" Alivia said loudly, jerking Rachel from her thoughts.

"Oh, ah, no." Rachel set the check on the desk next to the airline receipt. "I really can't keep this. I'll just leave it with you."

Alivia tried to push the airline receipt under another pile of papers, then moved the check toward Rachel. "I wish you'd take it. I've left enough money in Ariel's account to cover all outstanding checks. She'd really want you to have it."

"Well," Rachel hesitated. "I'm sure you have enough expenses to deal with. I'd hate to add to them."

At this, Alivia laughed. "You don't have to worry about that," she said lightly. "Ariel left me plenty of money to take care of everything. I inherited everything since her ex-husband is dead."

"Oh." Rachel was stunned that Alivia offered up this news so easily.

"In fact, I'm heading to the Bahamas to check on the house Ariel bought before she passed away. She purchased it without even going to see it. I'd hate to think someone tried to cheat her."

"I hope you're not going alone," Rachel said with concern. "Christmas is almost here. It would be sad to spend the holidays without your friends or family."

"I have no family left," Alivia said sadly. Her eyes slid to where the receipt had been. "But Adrian is going with me. I won't be alone."

Rachel hid her surprise. "That's good. It'll be nice for you to get away."

Alivia nodded, and when she did, a gold chain fell out from the folds of her shirt. Rachel stared at the golden sun pendant hanging from it.

"Oh! You're wearing Ariel's sun charm," Rachel blurted out.

Alivia's expression looked startled a moment, but then her face softened. "Ah, yes. It was my sister's favorite necklace. I feel closer to her when I wear it."

Rachel nodded her understanding. "That's sweet. I'm glad you have special mementos to remember her by."

"Well, I'm sorry I have to cut this short, but I have a lot to do," Alivia said, picking up the check. She held it in mid-air toward Rachel.

Rachel waved the check off. "Please keep it. I couldn't live with myself if I took it."

"Very well, then." Alivia set it back on the desk.

The two women walked together to the front door.

"I noticed you don't have the security camera up anymore,"

Rachel said as they stood in the open doorway.

Alivia frowned, looking annoyed. It made her look years older. "Yes. Since I won't be living here anymore, I saw no need for them."

"Of course," Rachel said. "Well, goodbye. Again, I'm sorry about Ariel."

Alivia's face softened, and she reached out and hugged a stunned Rachel. "Thank you, dear. And thank you for everything you've done for Ariel in the past." She pulled back. "I plan on keeping her books up for sale. And she did have a new manuscript ready to publish, so I'm sure I'll be contacting you soon for a cover."

"That's wonderful. I'm sure Ariel's readers will be happy to hear that," Rachel said. She hadn't realized Ariel had a new book ready to publish.

Alivia waved as Rachel walked away to her car.

* * *

On the long drive home, Rachel replayed the conversation with Alivia in her mind. She didn't know why it had bothered her. Alivia hadn't said or done anything suspicious. Rachel couldn't find fault with her selling the house so quickly. She wouldn't want to live in a home where a close family member had died under suspicious circumstances. And Alivia heading to the Bahamas wasn't that odd either. Who wouldn't want to go to a Bahama home over the Christmas holidays? She'd thought that Alivia had acted guilty when she'd realized Rachel had seen the airline receipt, but that could have been her imagination.

"I'm trying too hard to find something that isn't there," Rachel told herself. Alivia is just moving on with her life, and there was nothing wrong with that.

But still, some things bothered her. The thick coat of makeup on Alivia seemed strange. Rachel hadn't thought Alivia was the type to wear that much makeup, especially when she was just packing boxes around the house. And the way Alivia had moved easily in the high Espadrilles when she'd ran into the office. When Rachel had seen Alivia before, she'd worn flip-flops or sneakers.

But Rachel had to admit that she hadn't known Alivia all that well to begin with. Maybe all those things were her usual style after all.

"It's not my problem anymore," Rachel insisted out loud. "There's nothing more I can do." By the time Rachel had pulled into her driveway, she'd told herself to put all those thoughts out of her head.

Still, it was hard not to think about it.

As the days passed quickly leading up to Christmas, Rachel constantly found herself pondering everything Alivia had said to her. More than once, Rachel thought about calling Jack and running her thoughts past him to see what he thought. But she always stopped herself. After what he'd said to her the last time they'd seen each other—about how much he liked her—it would feel awkward to call him. She had no concrete evidence about anything, so it might seem as if she was looking for a reason to call him. Still, little things bothered her.

Alivia's whole demeanor had seemed odd to Rachel. Like her dramatic flair at the funeral as she spoke about her sister. It hadn't seemed like the way Rachel had pictured Alivia to behave. Then there was the way that Alivia kept calling her "dear" like Ariel had. And Alivia had hugged her goodbye—a gesture that would have been normal with Ariel but seemed awkward with Alivia. Rachel hardly knew her. Why would Alivia hug her?

Rachel knew she was being picky and silly. Still, it all bothered her. So, she kept all her thoughts to herself.

The Monday before Christmas, Rachel sat at her desk finishing up the last of her cover design projects for the year. She planned on taking two weeks off over the holidays so she could spend every moment with Avery.

As she closed her laptop, her phone buzzed. Rachel was surprised to see it was Rusty.

"Hi, Rusty," she said, smiling into the phone. "What a fun surprise to hear from you."

"Hey, there, little lady. I called because something strange has happened. I didn't know if the Lieutenant would want to know, so I thought I'd tell you first."

Rachel was intrigued. "What is it?"

"Pretty-boy sailed off earlier today. Remember all the stocking up of supplies he was doing? Well, today he left. He even came over and told me he was leaving for good."

"What?" Rachel was stunned. "Adrian left?"

"Yep. His slip is up for rent, and his boat is gone."

This news changed everything. Now Rachel knew that something was wrong.

CHAPTER SEVENTEEN

Rachel hurriedly thanked Rusty for calling her with the news about Adrian. She sat back in her chair, puzzled by what she'd just learned. Hadn't Alivia said that Adrian was flying to the Bahamas with her? If he wasn't, who was?

Once again, Rachel thought about her visit with Alivia. Putting the house up for sale so quickly, packing all the items even though it hadn't sold yet, and heading off to the Bahamas all seemed rushed. Rachel remembered staring into Alivia's green eyes. They'd been a vivid green. And the thick coat of makeup. It had seemed strange seeing Alivia wearing makeup while working around the house. And there was so much more that bothered Rachel. Like Alivia wearing the sun pendant that Ariel had loved so much. And Alivia calling her "dear" just as Ariel had done. Also, the magenta flowery top she'd worn that made her pale skin glow.

Rachel frowned. Pale skin glow. Alivia had enjoyed lying in the sun and tanning to the point of freckling. Hadn't Ariel complained about how her sister was ruining her skin?

Pale skin glow.

Rachel thought back to the day Ariel had fainted, and she'd

called Alivia in to help. Alivia had a golden tan that day. Ariel was the one with the porcelain skin.

Rachel knew something was terribly wrong. Quickly, she punched in Jack's number.

Jack answered on the second ring. "Hi, Rachel. I didn't think I'd be hearing from you so soon. What's up?"

Rachel hesitated. Jack sounded relaxed and casual as if nothing had happened between them. Maybe she'd taken it much more seriously than she should have.

"Hi, Jack. I just got a call from Rusty at the marina. He said that Adrian took off in his boat. He'd even told Rusty he was leaving for good. His slip is up for rent."

"That is news," Jack said, sounding unconcerned. "But I couldn't have been able to stop him anyway. The case is closed, and he has a right to leave."

"I realize that," Rachel said. "But there's something else I need to tell you. Do you have a moment to talk?"

"Sure."

Rachel could practically see his cocky grin, and it made her smile. "I went to visit Alivia last week."

"Really?" Jack's tone turned serious. "Why?"

"I wanted to return the check Ariel had given me, and I wanted to give her my condolences in person. We talked for a bit, and something I couldn't pinpoint kept bothering me. I saw a receipt for airline tickets on her desk—two tickets to the Bahamas."

"Okay. Hadn't Ariel purchased a house in the Bahamas? Maybe Alivia was going to check on it."

"That's what she said when she'd realized I'd seen the receipt. And it all makes sense, except for one thing. She bought two tickets. And she seemed nervous that I'd seen them."

"Maybe a friend is going with her," Jack said patiently.

"Yes. Alivia said Adrian was flying with her," Rachel told him.

"What?"

"I know. I didn't really think much of it then. But now that I know Adrian has left on his boat, who is flying to the Bahamas with Alivia? And why would she lie?" There was silence for a moment, and Rachel pictured Jack tapping his pencil on his notepad, thinking. In such a short time, she knew him well.

"Okay," he finally said. "Is there more that you're not telling me?"

Rachel took a calming breath. "I can't prove anything, but I picked up on a few things. Alivia has the house up for sale and was already packing items even though it hasn't sold. She also took the security cameras down. Maybe I'm crazy, but a man had been stalking her sister at the house. Wouldn't you want to keep the cameras up?"

"Yeah. That would be the logical thing to do. Unless Alivia is no longer afraid of the stalker," Jack said, his voice measured. "And that would make me believe she knew the stalker."

"That's what I thought," Rachel said. She was relieved she didn't sound like she was making up crazy ideas in her head. Jack was on the same wavelength.

"What else?" Jack asked.

"Okay. This sounds silly, but Alivia was wearing a lot of makeup even though she was at home, packing. I would have expected Ariel to wear that much makeup at home, but not Alivia."

"I agree. I always had the idea that Alivia was more casual," Jack said.

"What bothered me the most was Ariel complained how

her sister suntanned a lot, and it caused her to freckle, while Ariel was very careful with her skin. But yesterday, Alivia's skin was the same porcelain color as Ariel's. Alivia was golden tan just a couple of weeks ago. It doesn't make sense."

"Alivia wasn't tan at the funeral, either," Jack said. "I noticed that right away."

"Really? You noticed?" Rachel asked, surprised.

He chuckled. "I'm an investigator. I notice those things."

This made her smile.

"Seriously, though. I can't do anything just because she lied about her travel partner, and her skin isn't tanned. We need more," Jack said.

Rachel sighed. "I figured that. Still, it's all strange. Two people are dead, and the murderer is on the loose."

"But their deaths were ruled as accidents," Jack said.

"Do you believe that?" Rachel asked.

"Nope."

Rachel suddenly thought of something she hadn't told Jack yet. "I went to visit Rusty after the funeral last week. I wanted to see his footage of the woman who'd spent Thanksgiving weekend on Adrian's boat."

"I thought Alivia was with him that weekend," Jack said, sounding confused.

"That's what Adrian said. But remember how Rusty had seen a blond woman coming and going? I wanted to see the footage for myself," Rachel told him.

"Wait. Didn't Adrian explain that? He said that Alivia had dyed her hair blond to confuse the stalker."

"Yeah. And the woman in the video looks like she could be either Ariel or Alivia. It's hard to tell. But don't you think that's weird too? Why would Ariel want to put Alivia's life in danger by having them both look the same? And why would Alivia agree? And now, why isn't Alivia afraid of the stalker coming back?"

"What exactly are you getting at, Rachel?" Jack asked.

"I don't know. But Alivia and a companion are leaving the States tomorrow with a lot of money, and nothing is adding up. I feel like this case isn't over."

"I agree."

"You do?"

"Yes. And I think we have enough circumstantial evidence to at least stop them from leaving. But we'll have to grab them at the airport as they're trying to leave. Did you see what time the flight was for tomorrow?" Jack asked.

"It was an early flight to Miami, but I couldn't see what time the other flight to Nassau was," Rachel said.

"Okay. I'll do some checking. I'll call you later and let you know when I'll be picking you up," Jack said.

"Picking me up? Why?" Rachel asked.

"It's your hunch. Do you think I'm going to leave you out when we confront Alivia and her mystery traveler?" Jack gave a little laugh. "Then I can blame you if our hunches are wrong."

"Oh, gee. Thanks," Rachel said.

"I'll call you in a bit. Thanks for telling me everything. I think we're onto something." Jack hung up, leaving Rachel to wonder what he was planning. Could he actually have Alivia and her companion held up at the airport? And how embarrassing will it be if she and Jack were wrong about the whole situation?

Gritting her teeth, Rachel tried to finish up her cover project, but concentrating proved to be difficult.

* * *

The next morning, Rachel received a text from Jack asking her to meet him at the private plane area of the Tallahassee Airport by ten a.m. He'd texted her the night before to say things were in motion and he'd be in touch, and now she finally knew what he'd meant. Apparently, they'd be flying in a private plane to Miami International Airport.

Before leaving her house, Rachel considered calling Avery to tell him what was happening, but she decided against it. She knew he'd be busy wrapping things up at work so he could come the next day, and she didn't want to disturb him. Rachel also knew Avery was going to be upset with her for placing herself right in the middle of something that could be dangerous. She'd have to deal with all that after it was over.

Once at the airport, Rachel was directed to where the private planes landed, and she parked her car. She wasn't sure what to do next when she received a call from Jack.

"We're just landing now," he told her. "We need to top off the tank, and then we can take off. I'll come to get you in a minute."

As promised, Jack came out to the parking lot to find her.

"How on earth did you manage a private plane?" Rachel asked as he led her out toward the airfield.

He winked. "I have a few friends. I hope you don't get airsick in a small plane."

They rounded a hanger, and there sat a four-seater airplane.

"We're going up in that?" Rachel asked. It looked so small that she couldn't believe it could even fly.

"Yep. It's actually a really smooth ride. Come on. I'll introduce you to my friend," Jack said.

They walked up to the plane, and as Rachel drew closer, it looked even smaller. Rachel wasn't afraid of flying, but this plane was beginning to terrify her.

"Colby," Jack called out to the bearded man with a clipboard in hand. "This is Rachel."

Colby smiled and wiped his hand on his jeans before shaking hers. "Happy to meet you," he said. "We'll be off in a few minutes."

"I didn't know you had your own personal pilot," Rachel teased.

Jack grinned. "I went to college with Colby. He's actually a lawyer, but he also loves to fly. He's doing this as a favor for me."

"A lawyer?" Rachel said, surprised.

"How else do you think he can afford his own small plane?" Jack said with a wink. "I couldn't on my salary, that's for sure."

Colby waved for them to get inside. Rachel climbed into the back seat, and Jack sat in front with Colby. After buckling in, Colby offered Rachel a headset. "So, you can hear what's being said."

Rachel tensed as Colby maneuvered the small plane out toward the runway. Through the headset, she heard everything being said between Colby and the tower. He was finally told he could take off, and they made their way down the runway.

"Here we go," Colby said. He turned and smiled at Rachel just as the plane lifted off the runway. Soon, they were flying smoothly in the air above Florida.

"It's cool, right?" Jack's voice came over the headset.

"It is," Rachel said, looking out the window at the land below. "I've never flown so low I could see everything."

"It's beautiful up here," Colby said. "I could fly all the time if it would pay the bills."

After a few minutes of enjoying the view, Rachel finally asked, "Jack, what's the plan when we get there?"

"Plan?" Jack said. "I got the plane ride. Do I have to make up the plan, too?"

Rachel didn't need to see his face to know he had a silly grin on it. "Ha, ha."

"Seriously, though, I have a friend in Homeland Security who is going to be waiting for us at the airport. I checked, and Alivia's plane to Nassau doesn't leave until after three-thirty. They're going to let them go through security like everything is fine and then stop them as they get on the plane. If there's anything suspicious, they'll hold them there."

"And if there's nothing suspicious?" Rachel asked. She still questioned if her hunches were right.

"Then they are free to go, and I'll need to find a new job," Jack said jokingly.

"I hope you're kidding," Rachel said.

"Well, not really. But I believe our instincts are right. Something is wrong with this whole situation, and we're going to find out what it is," Jack told her. He turned in his seat and looked at her. "I believe in your instincts completely."

Rachel grimaced, which made Jack laugh.

"Don't worry. Everything will be okay," Jack said.

The flight took them about two hours, and Rachel worried the entire way. What if she'd been wrong? What if Alivia was just an innocent bystander, living her life. Randall could be dead, and Ariel may have died accidentally. But no matter how much she pondered it, she still saw a lot of holes in the stories.

It was one-thirty by the time their small plane landed, and they made their way to the main terminal. Colby went off to grab some lunch and wait for them.

"Do you want to eat anything before the big event?" Jack asked Rachel.

She stared at him as if he were crazy. "My stomach is in knots. I couldn't even think of eating. And what if Alivia and her travel friend see us? Won't that ruin everything?"

Jack laughed. "It's okay. They're way down on the other end of the terminal. If they are eating, it's far away from here. We'll ride with a security officer down there in a while." He led her to a small bar where they served food, and they sat in a back corner, just in case. Rachel only ordered a Coke, but Jack had a hamburger, fries, and a soda.

"Were you serious when you said you could lose your job over this?" Rachel asked, fiddling with the straw in her glass.

"Seriously? If I'm one-hundred percent wrong, I could be fired. The captain and I fought pretty hard over this. He's convinced nothing is wrong. I must have made a pretty strong case, though, because he wasn't completely convinced he was right. He said I could pursue this, but I had to let the authorities here handle it. And if Homeland Security thinks Alivia is fine, then I have to accept it."

"Your captain must really trust your instincts. That's good, right?" Rachel asked.

"Actually, he trusted your instincts. I told him some of the things you picked up on, and I guess it was enough to cause doubt." Jack smiled. "We make a good team, you and I."

Rachel was caught off guard by his words. She remembered Avery saying something similar when they were in California, solving the murder case together. *"We make a good pair,"* he'd said at one point. Rachel thought she and Avery made a good pair, too. That's why it surprised her that she and Jack also worked so well together.

Jack frowned. "Did I say something wrong?"

"No. I was just thinking. I hope things work out here and you don't lose your job. But that means I hope Alivia and her friend are murderers, and that isn't a great thought either."

Jack placed his hand over Rachel's. "It's going to turn out all right."

The touch of his hand made her even more nervous.

After Jack had eaten, he texted someone, and a few minutes later, as they left the restaurant, a security cart appeared.

"Our ride is waiting," he said to Rachel. "Let's do this."

Rachel nodded, and they got into the cart. She hoped they were doing the right thing.

CHAPTER EIGHTEEN

Rachel and Jack arrived one gate over from the flight to Nassau. They had to keep their distance, so Alivia wouldn't see them. They were on the very end of one of the terminals, so the Nassau plane was the only one this far down. At least there'd be fewer people in danger if things went sour.

Rachel watched as airport security officers casually made their way around the passenger area. Jack told her that the Miami Police were also nearby.

"They're going to wait until the other passengers have boarded before approaching Alivia and her companion," Jack said.

"How are they going to keep her from boarding without it looking suspicious?"

"I suppose they'll make some sort of excuse to keep them near the back of the line," Jack said.

"I would think they're already nervous. Won't that tell them something is up?"

Jack shrugged. "Let's hope not."

There were mirrors all over the terminal, and Rachel realized she could see Alivia and her companion sitting together as they waited for their flight. They didn't look nervous at all. She supposed since they'd breezed through security, they felt confident nothing would happen.

Rachel studied the man with Alivia. He wore jeans and a green polo shirt and looked tan. His hair was long, and he had a baseball cap over it, shadowing his face. She couldn't tell if it was Randall, but it definitely wasn't Adrian. The man was taller and more muscular than Adrian.

Rachel turned and nudged Jack, pointing to the mirror. He looked up and grinned.

"Good catch," he said, then placed his hand lightly on her back to turn her around. "We don't want them to see us," he explained.

She nodded.

More airport security officers came and stood near them, out of Alivia's view. The speaker overhead announced that their plane was now boarding. Rachel turned a bit to look in the mirror and saw Alivia and her companion head toward the front of the line.

"Here we go," Jack said. He looked at the mirror too. They watched as the woman taking tickets spoke to Alivia and motioned for her to move aside.

Rachel saw frown lines deepen on Alivia's face. She began arguing with the woman, and as she did, her voice rose high enough for Rachel to hear her.

"Everything's in order. We have first-class seats. Why can't we board?" Alivia complained. The man with Alivia patted her shoulder as if trying to calm her down, but she wouldn't stop. "No! We're boarding now!" She picked up her small carry-on suitcase and headed for the walkway. Instantly, a security guard was at her side, stopping her.

"Oh, no," Jack said, sounding worried. "This is escalating faster than we anticipated."

Rachel was so mesmerized by the scene in the mirror, she continued to watch. The security guard had led Alivia and her companion aside. Two more guards had joined them. Alivia was ranting and raving at the top of her lungs. In the midst of it all, Alivia glanced up and instantly stopped screeching. Her green eyes caught Rachel's brown ones in the mirrors.

"You!" Alivia screamed, pointing at the mirror. Her companion looked up and stared directly at Rachel too.

Rachel's heart pounded in her chest. They'd spotted her and Jack.

Chaos erupted. The security guards descended on Alivia and her companion as the passengers waiting in line scrambled to get out of the way. Jack told Rachel to get out of there fast, then he ran off with the other guards toward Alivia. Rachel watched as the large man with Alivia struggled with the guards and broke free. As he did, his hat and wig fell off, exposing his short hair. The man sprinted toward Rachel with guards chasing after him.

Rachel saw him coming and tried to flee, but he was too fast for her. The man grabbed Rachel, spun around, and put something cold against her neck. Everyone stopped as if frozen.

"Come near me, and this woman dies," the man said in a deep voice. Even through her terror, Rachel recognized his voice. It was the same man who'd claimed to be Randall in her backyard.

Rachel stood stock still, not daring to move. She saw Jack staring at her with fear in his eyes. Rachel realized in that second the man had a knife at her throat.

"You don't want to do this," Rachel said softly to the man.

"The con is over. They know who you are and what you've done." She had no idea who the man was, but she thought she might be able to get him to move away from her. "Killing me won't help you."

The man laughed in a guttural tone. "I don't need to kill you to get away," he whispered. "But they don't know that." He started to back away as the guards remained still. "Don't follow me," he barked at them. "Let me go and she'll stay alive."

Rachel tried to move along with him, but the blade pushed against her skin with every step. Cold fear ran through her. She didn't even dare to swallow for fear the movement would cause the knife to cut her.

Alivia pushed the guards away from her and walked toward Rachel and the man. "Randall, it's over. We're surrounded. You can't get away. Let Rachel go."

"Are you crazy?" Randall yelled. "Do you think this is a game? I will not spend the rest of my life in jail. I'm getting out of here."

Alivia drew closer. The guards behind her were inching their way toward Randall too. In a gentler voice, Alivia said, "This isn't Rachel's fault. We tried and we lost. Please. Don't make it any worse for us. It's over."

Randall shook his head. "No, Ariel. It's not over yet." He dropped the knife, spun, and sprinted down the corridor. Guards were already catching up to him before he made it too far.

Rachel stood still, not sure what had stunned her more. The fact that Randall was still alive and had tried to kill her or that the woman standing in front of her wasn't Alivia—she was Ariel.

"I'm sorry I dragged you into this," Ariel said sadly.

"Why, Ariel? Why did you do this?" Rachel asked.

She shook her head, and her red bob swished back and forth. "For the money, dear. Isn't that what it's always about?"

Jack rushed to Rachel's side as security guards and Miami Police officers surrounded Ariel. She was placed in handcuffs and walked down the corridor toward the spot where Randall had been pushed to the floor and cuffed.

"Are you okay?" Jack asked, studying the spot on her neck where the knife had been.

"I'm fine. Randall said he wasn't going to kill me, but that didn't make it any less scary," she told him.

Jack let out a heavy sigh. "You scared me to death. Thank God you're okay."

She smiled. "Were you afraid my FBI guy would come after you?"

"You bet." Jack grinned and placed his arm protectively around her shoulders. "How does it feel to be right about all this?"

"Sad," she said. "So many lives ruined, and for what? Money."

Jack nodded. "That's usually the driving force. Money, or jealousy."

She shook her head. "I don't know how you do it every day of your life."

"One day at a time," he said. "One day at a time."

Together they walked away down the terminal.

* * *

By the time Colby had flown Rachel back to Tallahassee, and she'd driven home, video of what had happened in Miami was all over the news. Jack had stayed behind to interview Ariel and Randall and to escort them back to the jail in Panama City Beach. Rachel had turned her phone off during the flight, and now, as she sat in the safety of her own home, she felt relieved that all had turned out fine.

"You could have been killed!" Avery said over the phone after Rachel finally turned it on and answered it. "Why were you there? What was that Lieutenant thinking, bringing you along?"

"It wasn't Jack's fault," Rachel explained patiently. "He told me to get out of there fast, and I hesitated. No one knew it would escalate that quickly."

Avery sighed. "You had a knife to your throat. The video is terrifying."

"I'm sorry," Rachel said. "I had no idea anyone was recording it and that it would hit the news that quickly, or else I would have called you. But I'm okay."

"Thank God," he said.

"You know what's strange? The knife to my throat wasn't the worst part of all this. It's the fact that Ariel and Randall killed people just to get the life insurance money. Ariel's own twin sister was killed so Ariel could be rich. That makes me sick just thinking about it," Rachel said.

"I'm sorry, sweetie," Avery said gently. "It's terrible what some people will do for money."

"I hope you're still coming tomorrow for the holidays," Rachel said. "I really need someone I love and trust with me right now."

"I'll be there," he said. "Just try and stop me."

Rachel smiled. She was so happy she had Avery in her life.

After she spoke with Avery, she called Jules and explained

what had happened. Her daughter had also seen the news story and had been terrified for her mother.

"I think you just like being on the national news," Jules teased her mother once she knew all was well. "You can't get enough of it."

Rachel laughed. "Believe me, I've had enough of it."

"Are we still going to Aunt Julie's for dinner tomorrow night?" Jules asked. It was only two days until Christmas.

"Yes," Rachel said. "No more sleuthing. No more danger. We're going to have a good old-fashioned Christmas with no murders."

"What fun is that?" Jules asked, her tone teasing.

"It's all the fun I need," Rachel assured her.

EPILOGUE

Avery arrived the next day and hugged Rachel so hard, he practically took her breath away—in a good way. She'd missed him so much, and considering the danger she'd been in just the day before, she appreciated Avery more than ever.

Avery stayed at the house while Jules and Rachel went to have dinner with Aunt Julie. Since Julie had never met Avery, they didn't want to upset her with a new face. Even though Julie couldn't remember either Rachel or Julie, she still seemed to have a good time having company for dinner and opening her presents from them.

"It's sad that Aunt Julie doesn't remember us anymore," Jules said as they walked out to their cars. "I feel like we've already lost her."

Rachel hugged her daughter tightly. "I feel that way too. But I think we made her happy tonight, and that's what's important."

Jules agreed. "I'll see you tomorrow for Christmas Eve dinner."

"You should plan to spend the night, too. We'll have a fun time," Rachel told her.

Jules shook her head and laughed. "No way. Not with you two love birds there. I'll give you some privacy."

Rachel laughed along. Her daughter was right, though. She couldn't wait to spend a lot of time alone with Avery.

The next day as Rachel was preparing side dishes to go with the grilled steak dinner they planned to eat that evening, there was a knock on her front door. Thinking that Jules had forgotten her key, she answered it and was surprised to see a familiar face.

"Jack! I thought you were my daughter."

He laughed. "Your daughter is a lot prettier than I am, that's for sure."

"What are you doing here? It's a far way to drive for a drop-in," Rachel said. She couldn't believe Jack was here, especially on Christmas Eve. But he looked happy and relaxed in jeans and a green sweater. Much different from two days ago with his dark suit and tense expression.

"Can I come in for a few minutes? I thought you might like to hear what happened with Ariel and Randall." Jack looked at her hopefully.

"Of course." She led the way to the kitchen and offered him a drink. "I have soda, wine, or beer."

"I wouldn't mind a beer," he said with a grin.

She gave him a bottle, and he declined a glass.

"I'm sorry to bother you on Christmas Eve. Honestly, I'd forgotten what day it was until I was halfway here. I hope I'm not disrupting your holiday."

"No, not at all. I was just getting things ready for dinner. Jules should be here any minute," Rachel said. "Let's go sit in the living room where it's more comfortable."

He followed her there, and just as they sat down, Avery

popped his head inside. He'd been outside getting the grill ready for dinner.

"Oh. Sorry. I didn't know you had company," Avery said.

"Join us." Rachel jumped up quickly. "This is Jack Meyers. Jack, this is Avery, my FBI guy." She chuckled.

Jack stood and offered his hand. "Nice to meet you."

Avery shook his hand. "Same here." He gave Jack the once-over. "I should probably be angry at you for putting Rachel's life in danger, but luckily it turned out okay."

"I'm sure I'm not the first person to pull Rachel out of a dangerous spot," Jack said with his cocky grin. "Or the last."

Avery stared at him a moment, then broke out laughing. "No, I guess you're not. But let's hope it's the last time."

"Hey, guys. I'm right here," Rachel said. "I can hear you, you know."

The men chuckled as Rachel shook her head at them.

"So, tell us, what did you learn about Ariel and Randall?" Rachel asked as they all sat down again.

"Randall wasn't as quick to admit to anything, but Ariel gave herself up pretty easily," Jack said. "You know how much she likes to talk about herself." He winked at Rachel.

She laughed. "That's the truth."

Jack sobered and was about to continue when Jules entered the room. After they greeted each other, Jack continued. "Ariel admitted it all. She and Randall had planned from the beginning to fake his death and then fake hers, too, to get the combined four million dollars. They'd even divorced to make it look like she had nothing to do with his death. Randall killed the homeless man at the marina and took samples of his hair so Ariel could place it in a hairbrush and say it was Randall's. That's how the man's DNA was misidentified."

Jules scrunched up her face. "Did Randall cut the man up so only his leg would come to shore?"

Jack nodded. "Yes. He knew the fire would destroy any blood evidence on the yacht."

"That's awful!" Rachel said. It made her sick just thinking about it.

"It is," Jack agreed solemnly. "But I think you suspected that was what he'd done." His brows rose at Rachel.

"Yes, but I was hoping I was wrong," she said.

"Did Ariel kill her sister? Or did Randall do it?" Jules asked.

"Ariel claims she was with Adrian when Randall drowned Alivia," Jack said. "Apparently Alivia had no idea what they were up to. She didn't even believe Randall was still alive. Ariel had asked her to dye her hair blond, and her sister did it to humor her. Of course, Ariel only wanted Alivia to do it so she could be identified as her."

Rachel shook her head. "That's so sad. She planned her own sister's death. I can't even fathom doing that for any amount of money."

"Some people are just that greedy," Avery said. "It's what keeps people like Jack and me busy."

"That's for sure," Jack said.

"So, it was Ariel who'd spent Thanksgiving weekend with Adrian," Rachel said. "That way she couldn't be implicated in her sister's death."

Jack nodded. "Yes. She didn't want to be at the house when Randall killed Alivia."

"Was Adrian in on it?" Jules asked.

Jack nodded. "I had put out an APB with the Coast Guard to find Adrian, but luckily, he had already come back on his own. He came willingly to the station yesterday with a lawyer and told us everything he knew. He admitted he'd followed Randall out into the Gulf so he could give him a ride back to shore after the yacht caught on fire. Adrian claims he had no idea that Randall had killed the homeless man until the leg appeared and was identified as Randall's. That's when Adrian got nervous. He didn't want to be an accessory to murder."

"Do you believe him?" Rachel asked.

"Yes. He let Randall stay on the yacht for a while, and that's why he'd cut his hair so short. Both he and Randall had the same haircut so no one would notice Randall coming and going. But after I searched the boat, Randall went to stay somewhere else. Adrian didn't know where," Jack said.

"Why did Adrian stay silent?" Jules asked. "He could have told you the truth and not gotten in deeper."

"He said he feared what Randall would do if he snitched on him. Randall had already killed one man. Adrian wasn't sure if their friendship would stop Randall from shutting him up for good too."

"And then there was Ariel," Rachel said. "I suppose Adrian kept quiet to protect her."

Jack nodded. "Yes. You called that one right, too. Adrian was in love with Ariel, and he believed Randall might hurt her. He thought he was protecting Ariel on Thanksgiving weekend until he learned Alivia was dead and was misidentified. He realized that Ariel was only using him and didn't really love him. That's why Adrian took off."

"Wow. All this for four million dollars," Rachel said. "It's insane. I suppose Ariel had thought she'd written the perfect murder mystery plot that no one would solve."

Jack grinned. "Except she did one thing wrong."

"What?" Rachel asked.

"She brought you into it. You were the one wild card she hadn't counted on."

Rachel frowned. "Why did she ask me to help when she knew all along what was going on?"

"You were supposed to be the one who'd help them get away with their plan," Jack said, giving her a sly grin. "She figured you'd believe that Randall was stalking her, and when she turned up dead, you'd go to the police with the story of the dead ex-husband who killed his ex-wife. Of course, no one would believe you, and the case would keep going in circles. Meanwhile, they'd be sitting on their deck in the Bahamas, sipping Bahama Mamas or whatever people drink there."

Avery laughed. "I guess Ariel didn't know you as well as she'd thought. Otherwise, she'd have known you'd see the tiny details everyone else missed."

"I guess she thought I was stupid or something," Rachel said, feeling insulted.

"Thank goodness she was wrong." Jules smiled at her mother. "Otherwise, two murderers would have gotten away."

The others agreed. It was good knowing that they'd be brought to justice.

Jack stood. "Well, I should be going so you can enjoy your Christmas Eve." He looked at Rachel. "Thank you for helping with this case. You blew it wide open. I owe you one."

Rachel laughed. "You don't owe me anything. And from now on, I'm staying away from interesting murder plots. If anyone calls me with a problem, I'm hanging up immediately."

"Well, that would be a shame," Avery said, draping his arm lovingly over her shoulders. "You do such good work."

She smiled at him, her heart warmed by his sweet gaze.

Jack cleared his throat, looking embarrassed by their display of affection. "It's time for me to go."

Avery stood. "Why don't you stay for dinner? Unless you have other plans," he said, glancing over at Rachel.

She nodded agreement, although she was surprised Avery had invited him. "Yes. Stay. We have plenty."

Jack looked hesitant. "Are you sure? I don't want to impose."

"You're not imposing. Stay. You and Avery can talk shop. He loves discussing his cases," Rachel said.

The foursome had a lovely evening with lively conversation. After Jack and Jules had left, Avery helped Rachel clean up the kitchen, and then they went into the living room to sit by the lit Christmas tree.

"Jack seems like a great guy. Very knowledgeable," Avery said. He gave her a sly grin. "But are you sure he doesn't have a thing for you?"

"Oh, stop. You and Jules have vivid imaginations. We worked well together, but that was all." At least that was all she would tell Avery. Rachel rose up and kissed him lightly on the lips. "It's nothing like you and me. We bonded in other ways."

"We did." Avery kissed her again, this time deeper. Then he grinned.

"What's that silly grin for?" she asked, pulling back.

"Were you serious about never helping with a murder mystery again?"

"Absolutely," she said with determination. "No more sleuthing for me."

Avery laughed and bent to kiss her again. "We'll see."

The End

ABOUT THE AUTHOR

Deanna Lynn Sletten loves a good murder mystery. As a child, she was fascinated by her great-uncle's job as a forensic scientist for the Los Angeles County Sheriff's Department. Her first chapter books were *Nancy Drew Mysteries* and she could never say no to an Agatha Christie novel. It's also not surprising that she loves watching true-crime stories on television. So, it was only a matter of time that Deanna would try her hand at writing a murder mystery.

Deanna has been writing novels since 2011 and is always up for a challenge. She writes women's fiction, romance, historical fiction, and now murder mysteries. She lives in northern Minnesota with her husband and has two grown children. Her favorite thing to do is walk the wooded trails around her home with her new little Aussie puppy.

Learn more at: deannalsletten.com

Printed in Great Britain
by Amazon